THE

CW01648303

I GOT THIS
BOOK FOR
MY BIRTHDAY
2015

By the same author in Pan Books

KILL JASON KING!

THE PROTECTORS

Based on screenplays by Dennis Spooner,
Brian Clemens and Ralph Smart

ROBERT MIALL

A PAN ORIGINAL

PAN BOOKS LIMITED : LONDON

First published 1973 by Pan Books Ltd,
33 Tothill Street, London, SW1.

ISBN 0 330 23473 0

*Printed and bound in England by
Hazell Watson and Viney Ltd,
Aylesbury, Bucks*

CONTENTS

Part One
THE BODYGUARDS
page 7

Part Two
DISAPPEARING TRICK
page 51

Part Three
THE NUMBERS GAME
page 97

Part One

THE BODYGUARDS

I

The shadowy face of the driver was as dusky and impenetrable as the barriers of trees beside the road. Moonlight stabbed fitfully across the silver bonnet of the Rolls-Royce, and occasionally touched an upper window or the gable end of some large mansion set well back in its sheltering woodland. The car purred on, the driver impassive, his two passengers silent.

There was no point in wasting words on mere guesswork. And guesswork it would have to be until they reached their destination.

Harry Rule glanced at his companion.

The moonlight, clear of clouds and trees for a moment or two, struck a faint auburn glow from her hair. She was settled comfortably with her head back – relaxed but not lolling, resting but not asleep. Caroline, he thought enviously, was a great one for resting: like an especially sleek, sensuous cat she could drowse warmly right up to the moment when she needed to spring. That Italian marriage of hers had taught her a beautiful balance between passion and repose.

Again the shadows closed in. Branches interlaced above the road.

Harry leaned forward. 'You're sure we're on the right road, Chino?'

The speed of the car did not falter by as much as one inch per hour. The reproachful answer had all the dour melancholy of Chino's olive eyes.

'We shall reach the exact place at the exact time. There will be a gatehouse on the next corner but two, we shall turn right, and one hundred yards down the road we shall be there.'

'Sorry.' Harry let himself sag back into his seat again.

The Contessa opened one eye and smiled to herself.

They were driving through an eerie, unreal world. London was far behind yet they were not truly in the country. The estates on either side, the coppices and parklands and occasional high walls, were not those of working squires or even of the gentry who had once owned most of this county. Today the original manors and some newer creations belonged to pop stars with a yearning to get away from it all – but not too far away – and to property developers who preferred to keep a sylvan distance between themselves and their crimes. An oil company magnate opened his garden to the public twice a year; a millionaire art collector refused to open even his front door; and a retired financier with more enemies than was healthy for any one man was said to have installed a moat and drawbridge, which was raised every night.

The Rolls-Royce slowed and turned by a gatehouse, just as Chino had promised. Further down the lane was a curve of stone wall, broken by two massive gateposts.

Harry had half expected someone to be on duty at the gates, but they were open. Chino drove up the gravel drive, and rustled to a halt before the house.

The Contessa yawned gently, but was wide awake as she stepped out on to the gravel.

Harry Rule was more familiar with the architecture of the Western seaboard and of New England than with that of the older England. But he had carried out enough assignments here now to recognise certain styles. He knew what they called Stockbroker's Tudor when he saw it. He'd have hated, though, to have to put a name to this looming pile. Brewer's Gothic, maybe. It was heavy and lumpy, with phoney mullioned windows and a couple of crazy turrets against the moon-raked sky. The porch could have served a Victorian railway station.

The Contessa said : 'If Boris Karloff opens the door, I'm off.'

Harry tugged the handle of an ancient bell chain. A rasping and scraping within the wall was followed by a distant jangle.

Slow footsteps took an age to reach the door.

Then a stooped, deferential butler stood in the opening. Behind him a vista of humped shapes enveloped in dust sheets undulated away towards a grandfather clock, its moon face smirking at the visitors.

'Mr Rule?'

'And the Contessa di Contini.'

The butler bowed even lower. 'The gentleman is waiting for you upstairs, sir. The second door on the right.'

Harry led the way to a staircase which curved up to a balustraded landing. Their feet made no sound on the heavy pile of the stair-carpet. The house felt dead, unlived-in; and the shrouded furniture in the hall below became a cluster of crouching ghosts.

The second door on the right, flanked by sombre portraits of a family long since bought up and sent packing, was slightly ajar. Harry rapped on it with two knuckles.

'Come in.'

He stood back to let the Contessa enter, and followed her through.

The room was lit only by candles. Mysterious darkness lurked in the corners, pulsing as each conflicting draught set the flames swaying and dipping. Set with its head to one wall was a four-poster bed with rich brocade hangings. It was an inappropriate frame for the man in a raincoat who perched on the edge, snipping away at his nails with a small pair of clippers.

'Newman,' said Harry curtly.

He had worked with the man once or twice before. And also clashed with him before. Until Newman came out with what was on his mind this time, conversation was best kept nice and cool and offhanded.

Newman said: 'Thanks for coming.'

'You made it sound urgent.'

'It is. We want to hire you.'

The police, guardians of law and order, wanting to hire free-lance operators in the same field . . .?

'As bodyguards,' Newman added.

The Contessa was staring at another feature of the room.

It wasn't what you'd call a particularly desirable item of bedroom furniture.

It was a coffin. And the lid was off.

Caroline moved closer. As she let out a little gasp, the candles at each end of the coffin wavered, their light intensifying the dark gashes in Newman's bleakly chiselled face.

'And why should Ralph Corder require *our* services?' The Contessa was staring down into the waxen face of the corpse.

'You pride yourselves' – Newman pushed himself away from the bed and came to stand beside her – 'on being the world's best bodyguards. Well, here's a body for you to guard.'

'You haven't answered the lady's question,' said Harry. 'If that's Ralph Corder in there—'

'It is.'

'So?'

'Very simple.'

'Make it more so.'

'We have every reason to believe,' said Newman, 'that someone is going to try and kill him.'

2

Protection rackets had never appealed to Harry Rule. He had always been distinctly unfriendly towards men in New York, Chicago and points West who collected regular fees to ensure that they themselves would not lob petrol bombs and other such devices through the windows of certain saloons, shops and clubs. In Europe he came across more subtle methods; but the game was the same, and it wasn't a game he thought should be played too often. His own interpretation of the word 'protection' was quite different. Over the years the conviction grew on him that there was a need for the real thing.

Pretty rough years, looking back on them. Years of trying to stay clean even when you had to fight dirty.

At the start he'd got a kick out of whatever job came along; enjoyed being paid, and enjoyed pitting his wits and a whole lot of things more violent than his wits against the toughest villains around. He got a special pleasure out of removing the worst specimens from circulation. And when some of them got back into circulation and came looking for him, he didn't mind that either: danger was a good stimulus.

But after a while the taste began to go sour. A private detective had to accept plenty of commissions that didn't smell too good – and stank more and more as they went on. If you were in business, you were in business. You couldn't pick and choose.

Or could you . . .?

Harry Rule reached the stage when he had to choose. If he wasn't going to spend the rest of his working life with bad fits of indigestion, he had to get away from the unsavoury routine stuff – the bitter divorce cases, the high-priced snooping for industrialists who made noble speeches at big conventions and let other men tackle their less conventional requirements, the political jobs, and the guard-dog assignments for wheeler-dealers who'd be a lot better thrown to the wolves.

He was no starry-eyed idealist, but he did want to be able to live with himself. And, along the way, keep a few other citizens alive.

There were people really in need of protection. Real protection, by experts who had learnt the hard way.

Experts ... he was beginning to think in the plural.

Harry didn't exactly recruit Paul Buchet. The two of them came together after a rough-house in Marseilles and found they talked the same language. If Paul's accent was slightly different from his own, that was no handicap. Paul heard different nuances, saw different possibilities, complemented Harry's techniques with his own. He had spent a long time in the specialized field of industrial espionage, and now found it distasteful. His skills were at the disposal of anyone who wanted to clean up the world; or simply to clean up some grubby little personal situation. He was a one-man insecticide of the electronic bug world.

'The Protectors,' Paul had agreed. 'Yes, I think that is how it must be. We will protect. We will defend those in need.'

'And if the best form of defence is attack ...'

'Then we shall attack, no?'

They had laughed about it, tossed it to and fro, and laughed about the notion of issuing a high-flown prospectus. *We protect those in peril ... results guaranteed or money back ... no risk too great ... no assignment too challenging.* And then stopped laughing as they realized that they were in earnest. This was what it was all about. This was exactly how it was going to be.

There were no formalities. No deeds of association. No glass doors with gilt lettering. No brash advertising.

Which didn't mean they were unprofessional. Or free and easy. They were rarely free, often expensive. And they were hard rather than easy – hard in their standards, hardest of all to themselves.

When the Contessa di Contini came into the organization,

Harry did wonder whether she was not too amateurish. Adorable, but an amateur.

How she actually came to join them, he could never quite explain. His memory was usually a good match for any of the electronic devices Paul played with. Years later he could conjure up a name once heard or a face once seen : useful in his work, bad luck on any number of shady characters scattered across the United States and Europe. But whenever he asked himself just how Caroline appeared on the scene, he got a different picture each time.

Maybe it was because of the blow he'd had on the head just before meeting her. If she hadn't dragged him out of the Tiber that time, he'd have been in no position to remember anything, anyway.

Or maybe his mind was hazed by her bewildering habit of popping up, popping off, and showing up just as unpredictably as she had gone, with some risky deed neatly tidied up and some insoluble problem shrewdly solved.

The Contessa had developed not so much as a private eye as a private ear. And a very acute ear at that. Her late husband's friends had always found her a sympathetic listener. She was a discreet adviser and an equally discreet investigator. The husky laugh set people at ease. They told her more than they knew they were telling. She was a diplomat rather than a detective. She knew where to make the right contacts; knew where personal problems got too big and too impersonal for one person to handle; and, infuriatingly, usually knew someone powerful enough to get her out of trouble when the crunch came.

An adventuress, thought Harry sometimes. Not the golddigging kind – she already had enough of that – but a beautiful, talented woman who liked adventure.

Other so-called security services used armour-plated cars and hefty bruisers with hefty truncheons. Harry, Paul and Caroline relied on know-how, cunning, and their own zest for the tricky sorting out of tricky situations.

They were the Protectors.

3

'But protecting a dead man . . . !' The Contessa shook her exquisite head. 'Why? And why us?'

'Answer to the first question,' said Newman: 'some of his old friends don't know he's dead. It's something they'd very much *like* to know.'

'I don't get that. Maybe if you answer the second, we'll be able to sort it all out.'

'You're getting a reputation,' said Newman grudgingly. He was like a regular Army officer forcing himself to be polite to an unpredictable guerrilla group he had to enlist as an ally. 'Word's getting around where it matters.'

'Unsolicited testimonials, no less,' observed Harry.

'Our informers tell us' – the CID man was piling it on – 'that some of the muscle boys turn pale when they hear you've been hired for the opposition.'

'Isn't he sweet?' cooed Caroline.

'So that if you show up somewhere, it means business.'

Harry blinked. It must be the uncertain moonlight outside, followed by the smoky flicker of the candles in here, that made everything so hazy.

He made an effort. 'Look, this still doesn't add up. We're known to some of the heavies as a good defence team. Right. They prefer not to tangle with us. So when they know we're here, guarding a dead body, they'll be frightened off. And will you tell me why you want them chased away from a corpse?'

'We don't!'

'I must have missed something,' said Harry despairingly.

'We want to flush 'em out. I've said you scare some of them. But not all. Not enough to put them off altogether. Not when there's something really big involved.'

'Really big?'

Newman resumed work on his nails, clipping away with

all the ardour of a suburban householder trimming his privet hedge. He said: 'If you're here, and known to be here, they'll think Corder's still alive. And they'll just have to get to him.'

'And we nab them on the way in?'

'That's about the size of it.'

Harry edged closer to the Contessa, who was still casting the occasional disturbed little glance down at the dead white mask of a face in the coffin.

'Corder was quite a distinguished financier,' he ventured. 'Who's so keen to get at him?'

'He was distinguished,' said Newman grimly, 'by his flair for removing large sums of money from banks.'

'That's what I said – a distinguished financier.'

'I mean that he sent his yobboes in to bash in the odd safe or two, and to beat a few bank clerks over the head.'

'Not that Islington robbery last year?'

'Among others.'

'The fifty thousand from Hatfield?' Caroline suggested.

'That one, too, most likely. We're not sure of all the ramifications. But we're sure it was Corder behind it. What we're not sure of ...' Newman stopped chipping at his nails and bit his lip.

'Yes?' Harry prompted.

'We don't know where the money is. And we're not sure who worked with him. We'd like to settle the two things at one go.'

'And we're the sacrificial goats?'

'There's nothing to be afraid of.'

'Afraid?' Caroline burst out indignantly.

'I've explained why we want you here – showing yourselves on the terrace, wandering around, letting them know you're on the premises. But you won't be in any danger. My men will—'

'Your men will do precisely nothing,' said Harry. 'Nothing at all, until we tell them.'

'Now look here. We're hiring you, but—'

'If we're hired, we do it our way. Or not at all.'

'We only want you—'

'As decoy ducks. Yes, I know.'

'Quite a menagerie of metaphors,' marvelled the Contessa.

'But that's not how we operate,' said Harry. 'We take the job, we do the job our way. You want Corder's accomplices and you want the loot. Stay out from under our feet, and you stand a chance of getting delivery.'

'The Commissioner won't like this.'

'An ungrateful oaf, the Commissioner,' said Harry.

'If anything goes wrong—'

'Leave it to us.'

Newman left it to them.

When he had gone, they sent Chino to put the Rolls away and report on the position of the garage, old stables and any other out-houses. A more detailed recce could be carried out in the morning. Quite apart from seeing more of the grounds for themselves, they would also be seen – if anyone was looking.

'And we'd better ring Paul,' said Harry. 'If the phone in this mausoleum is in working order.'

The butler, summoned by means of an embroidered bell-pull, showed them the telephone in an embrasure designed by the architect to look like a priest's hiding hole.

Paul Buchet proved to be in bed in his Paris flat. It was difficult to tell from his grumblings whether he had company or whether he was simply grouchy at being dragged from his slumbers.

He agreed without noticeable enthusiasm that if he got up now he could catch a plane which would land him at Heathrow just after dawn. Chino would be sent to collect him.

'And make yourself as conspicuous as possible,' said Harry.

'Conspicuous? What kind of job is this?'

'We'll tell you over breakfast.'

A late breakfast on the terrace, thought Harry: on the terrace, for the whole world to see.

The butler showed them to their bedrooms.

Newman had evidently taken it for granted that they

would accept the commission. However shrouded and musty the rest of the house might be, these two rooms had been aired, and the linen was crisp and fresh-smelling. A small coal fire flickered cheerfully in each grate.

There was, the butler confirmed, one housemaid still in residence : 'A very capable girl, sir. Not one of your modern flibbertigibbets. She'll turn her hand to a good breakfast, I promise you.'

Harry lay awake for almost an hour, listening to the shiftings and creakings of the house. His room was immediately above the funereal chamber. The double-glazed windows there had been tightly fastened. He had double-checked the locks and bolts around the ground floor, though he didn't really expect anyone to start operations tonight. Only when the alarm was raised – when Corder's associates knew the Protectors were here in force – was an attack likely.

But when at last he fell asleep, it was a light sleep. The faintest alien sound from below would have woken him.

The morning was bright and clear. A man watching from the slope above the lane, or from the main road turning into the trees on a crest to the south, would be able to see two people on the terrace. With binoculars he would have no difficulty in identifying those two people. And unless he was singularly unobservant he could scarcely miss the slow progress of the Rolls downhill towards the turn-off, its hesitation on the corner while Paul Buchet put his head out of the window to study the landscape, and its majestic entry between the two gateposts and on up the drive.

Then there were three on the terrace.

Explanations over and breakfast over, they set to work. Paul found a pair of step-ladders and climbed up to install a camera within the canopy of the four-poster, angled down on Corder's coffin but taking in the door of the room as well. Then he fitted an electronic eye to the door frame. Three times the Contessa walked in and out, and three times the eye triggered the camera shutter. Paul checked the prints, and adjusted the camera. Nobody now could walk between the door and the coffin without being recorded.

They didn't want the elderly butler running any risks. To his great indignation – respectfully but quiveringly expressed – they substituted Chino. It had to be admitted that he was far from convincing: his features were rather darker than one would have expected in this corner of the Home Counties, and his broad shoulders threatened to split the seams of the shiny black coat he struggled into. But it didn't matter if he made visitors suspicious. The fishier the set-up, the more anxious Corder's old chums would be to get in and investigate.

The Contessa slowly and deliberately drew all the curtains back from windows at the front of the house. Each time she stood in the window looking out for a minute or two.

Harry Rule paced out the grounds, assessed vantage points, and calculated the fastest getaway they could manage if the Rolls had to set off in pursuit.

In pursuit of whom... of what?

It was a waiting game.

When he had finished at the back of the house, Harry went indoors through the kitchen and along a passage ending in a baize-padded door. It opened into the hall. He stepped in among the white-sheeted hummocks of furniture.

There was something else white – something which had not been there earlier this morning. It was an envelope in the wire cage of the letter-box.

'Chino!'

Hobbling rather than walking upstairs, the new butler turned carefully to look down, gasping at the pressure of his waistband.

'How long has that letter been there?' Harry demanded.

Chino stared; shook his head.

The Contessa came along the landing. 'What's the matter? Corder's final demand for income tax, maybe?'

Harry lifted the wire lid and took out the envelope. There was no stamp on it. No full address. Simply his own name: Harry Rule.

'Not even an "Esquire",' said the Contessa, descending the stairs and weaving her way through the dust-sheets. 'Not even a "Mr".'

Harry opened the door. There was nobody on the drive. He stepped out, and looked to left and right. Nobody on the lawns. The slight breeze stirred the bushes. Somebody had come fast and gone fast.

He tore open the envelope.

There was one sheet of paper inside. The message was brief:

> *If you want to make an easy five*
> *thousand meet George at two o'clock*
> *by Cleopatra's Needle.*

'*Do* you want an easy five thousand?' asked the Contessa brightly.

'What I really want,' mused Harry, 'is to know whether it's a straightforward bribe or whether they merely want to get me out of the way.'

'There's only one way to find out.'

4

When Harry had driven off, deliberately coaxing more noise from the Rolls' engine than the manufacturers would have approved, the Contessa continued her detailed inspection of the interior. From time to time she showed herself at a window, and saw Paul going over the same ground outside which Harry had already explored.

He ran the risk of a bullet in the back, of course. She felt a twinge of apprehension. But the invaders, when they came, would surely want to keep violence to a minimum. They weren't going to invite a murder charge. The only person in danger of sudden death would have been Ralph Corder; and Corder was far beyond that now.

She passed Chino in a corridor.

'Everything quiet?'

They nodded at each other. A couple of watchmen doing their rounds, she thought.

She went up a flight of back stairs to another landing, and looked out. There was no sign of Paul now. He was probably going through the stables, or investigating the bushes.

Suddenly, from below, she heard a faint but insistent buzz.

The Contessa hurried back the way she had come, and back to the room where Corder lay in his coffin. They had screwed the lid back on, and the candles were out. The buzz came steady and louder now from the bureau against one wall. She opened the flap. A light was winking on the panel of the electronic unit which Paul had fitted inside. It must have been set off by one of the bugs plugged into the trees nearest the house.

She switched off the warning, and closed the flap.

Chino had reached the doorway.

'Is Paul still outside?'

'Yes, Contessa.'

'I think we have a visitor.'

They went out, to the head of the stairs. Chino began to move cautiously down. Caroline went to the back stairs. It was possible that a door could have been forced below, or that someone had come in through the old, disused scullery. She hesitated, trying to cover both directions at once.

There was the creak of a board.

The Contessa edged away from the stairs and into an alcove which might once have held a chair or an occasional table.

A dark silhouette crossed the window at the end of the landing.

She heard the door of Corder's room open.

There was an interminable silence. Then a swift succession of muffled plops. It was an odd, spongy sound, but one which she recognized immediately – the sound of a silenced revolver.

Who was he firing at?

'Chino!' she shouted.

The dark shape spun across the window again, veered, and came towards her. The gun was raised. She could just make out the twisted features of the man, scared and twitching, against the diffuse light. Then Chino had launched himself from the angle of the landing.

The two men went down. The gun skidded away. Chino got up, his hand swinging in a savage chop. But the gunman ducked, scrabbled a few feet desperately on his hands and knees, and lurched away. As Chino regained his balance, a splintered chair crashed across his path.

Caroline ran to join him. They kicked the chair aside, and rushed down the main staircase as the front door slammed shut.

By the time they had wrenched it open again, the intruder was well on his way towards the gate. A few seconds later they heard him revving a car, and the whine as it gathered speed up the lane to the junction.

'Paul...?'

Chino went out over the grass. The Contessa went back up to Corder's room, dreading what she might find. Of course Paul hadn't been there a few moments ago, when she went in to switch off the alarm. But had he, too, heard it and dashed in there just after she had left? Those shots . . . they had been fired at *somebody*.

The door was open. She went in.

A ragged pattern of holes in the side of the coffin made it look as if someone had been punching air-holes in the woodwork, to enable the occupant to breathe. But Corder wasn't doing any breathing. If he'd been breathing before, he certainly wouldn't have been much good at it now.

They really must have the jitters, this crowd. To pump bullets wildly into a coffin . . .

If they got that hysterical that easily, there was no telling what they might do next.

The Contessa returned thoughtfully to the hall in time to see Chino entering with Paul Buchet slung over his shoulder.

'He's all right? They haven't . . . ?'

She tugged a sheet away from an oak settle, and they lowered Paul on to it. He was breathing hoarsely. As Chino propped his head against the knobbly end of the settle, his eyes opened. He winced, closed them again; then blinked and groaned and forced himself to sit upright.

'Somebody hit me,' he announced.

'I'll get some cold water.'

'And some whisky to put in it, please.'

'I'll ring for the butler.'

'I am the butler,' Chino reminded her.

'Then go and see what's in your pantry. Or in the cellar, or wherever.'

Paul probed the back of his head with his fingers.

'Did you see who it was?' asked the Contessa.

'No. I sensed there was somebody out there – in the bushes along the west wall, I thought. But then I thought it was my imagination.'

'And it wasn't.'

'It was not,' said Paul ruefully. Then he got to his feet. 'Did he get into the house?'

'Right into Corder's room.'

'Did we get a picture?'

'You'd better come and see.'

He swayed. As she steadied him, he said: 'And what do you suppose is happening to Harry? All a wild goose chase?'

'First sacrificial goats,' laughed Caroline. 'Then decoy ducks. And now wild geese!'

5

Big Ben tolled out the strokes of two o'clock above the rumble of Embankment traffic. Harry Rule looked up at the spike of Cleopatra's Needle, leaned back against the parapet, and studied the passers-by. Eager faces, peevish faces, blank faces: most of them ignoring him, a few looking at him curiously or incuriously; one girl with an arrogant tilt to her nose glaring at him in the belief that he was about to make a pass at her.

A young man dawdled along and halted a few feet away. Harry tried to decide whether he was the sort of young man whose name could be George.

But he was moving on.

A dog barked. It was a friendly, untroubled bark. The animal's lead was tied to the leg of one of the nearby seats. An odd place to leave a dog, thought Harry abstractedly. Where was the owner – having a quick lunch at the Savoy?

The dog barked again, and wagged its tail as a man in a shabby grey suit nipped in and out of the traffic and reached the pavement. Harry tensed. But the man went past, on towards Waterloo Bridge.

Minutes ticked by. Harry looked at his watch; and looked at it, obsessively, again and again.

His guess had been right. He had been lured here simply to get him out of the way. He could only hope that Paul and Caroline would be able to deal with whatever hit them. They were good. Very good. But when there was action, Harry had an itch to be right on the spot himself.

The dog was panting eagerly, its tongue out. Harry took a few paces to and fro, and stooped to pat the shaggy head.

Then he froze.

The name tag on the collar was clearly lettered. Like the envelope he had received this morning, it carried no address. Just the name: George.

'You're in it too, eh?' said Harry softly. He unfastened the lead from the seat. 'Crime's no life for a dog, George.'

George's tail began to wag furiously. As soon as he was freed, he began to pull Harry along the Embankment. Harry had no idea where he was going; but George had.

It was quite a walk, but the dog didn't falter. They climbed the steps to Waterloo Bridge and trotted to the south side of the river. Harry was prepared to be led into some shabby side street or, even more likely, one of the alleys between the Bankside warehouses. Instead, he was taken into an unexpected oasis of dusty green, overlooked by gaunt tower blocks of new flats.

The area could hardly be called a park. There were a few flower beds, but the flowers had been trampled by neighbourhood kids and, probably, less well disciplined dogs than the amiable George. Four paths intersected at the middle, where there was a circle of seats. Other seats were set along the paths, and beyond low railings was a road. The patch of green stank of petrol rather than of would-be countryside.

George padded towards an unoccupied bench, and sat down beside it. His tongue drooped out. He panted happily.

'Is this it, George?'

George cocked his head.

'Still not talking, eh?'

Harry tied the lead round the arm of the bench, and sat down.

Pop music drifted along the path from another seat, some twenty yards away. Two girls sat with their heads back, one fair and one dark, jerking in time to the music. They both had long legs – and attractive legs. Both had their right legs crossed over the left, and their feet twitched a conflicting tempo.

It was distracting. Harry looked away.

An elderly man crossed the gardens on the far side, and disappeared. Several housewives with shopping baskets dawdled near the railings, chatted, and then went on their way.

George sat patiently where he was. Harry sat less patiently.

A sports car whined round a corner and came to a halt by a gate behind Harry's bench. He looked over his shoulder. A young man with a scarlet shirt and mauve slacks got out. He looked very sure of himself. There was a mark down one cheek which might be an old scar – the scar, it could be, of a razor slash.

Harry braced himself, ready to get on his feet in a hurry if he had to.

But the newcomer was paying no attention. He leaned on the railings and whistled, and when the girls' heads turned he waved to them.

They laughed, and one shouted something; and they both got up.

It wasn't really the right setting for them. They belonged somewhere smarter, somewhere noisier.

The girls were running now, piling into the sports car, shrieking as the man put his arms round both of them and then let them go, sliding in behind the wheel and yelling a whole lot of boisterous nothingness.

It was not until the car began to draw away that Harry realized the music was still pounding out across the grass.

He jumped up. 'Hey – your radio!'

Tyres screeched at the corner, and the sports car was gone.

George wagged not only his tail but his whole bottom, squirming it into the path, snuffling up at Harry as if to ask what all the fuss was about.

The music cut out suddenly, in the middle of a bar.

Harry stared at the transistor where it lay, tilted against the back of the bench.

A metallic voice said, precisely and clearly: 'Hello, Harry.'

George obviously recognized the voice. He tugged at the lead until it was a thrumming, tight line, straining to reach the other bench.

Harry walked to the bench and stood over the radio.

'Sorry for the dramatics,' it crackled at him, 'but they were essential.'

He picked it up, looked at it, and looked up at the dizzy piles of flats. What was the range of the thing – and was somebody up there at one of those windows, watching his reactions?

'This receiver is two-way. I can hear you.'

Harry said: 'What is it you want?'

'I like that, Harry. Direct. To the point.'

'Let's have some of that in return, then. Direct and to the point.'

'Take a look in that litter basket.'

Harry glanced along the bench to the wire basket at the end. It was heaped with the usual mixture of ice-cream wrappers, crumpled cigarette packets, and shreds of newspaper.

'You'll find a parcel inside.'

Holding the radio in one hand, he rooted with the other. In the middle of the loose bits and pieces was a more substantial bulk. He pulled it out. A double sheet of newspaper was wrapped round something.

'I've got it.'

'Open it, then.'

Harry opened it. Enclosed in the paper were two plump wads of five-pound notes. Or, rather, of half notes. They had all been sliced neatly in two.

'Five thousand pounds, Harry. I have taken the precaution of keeping half of them. You can collect the balance if you can prove the answer to a simple question.'

'I'm listening.'

'Is Ralph Corder dead?'

A car went past. A jet described a long arc across the sky. Two women with children came in through the gate, and the children scampered across the grass. Harry waited until they were well past.

And then went on waiting.

'Well?' demanded the voice.

Harry said: 'I'd like the other end of these notes.'

'I'm sure you would. And you shall have them. When you've answered my question. *And* proved it.'

'How do I do that?'

'I leave that to you. But I want positive proof. No clever stuff, Harry.'

Harry Rule hesitated. Then he said: 'How do I contact you?'

'You don't. Tell me where you'll be, and when you can come up with the goods, and I'll be in touch.'

'I may be out in the country part of the time,' said Harry tentatively.

'At Corder's place? I'll try there.'

'Or I may have to spend some time in London. I'm not sure.'

'I'll ring your flat.'

'I'm not listed.'

'You don't have to be.' The chuckle was like some bird croaking. But there were no birds in these dried-up gardens. 'I know your number, Harry. I know a lot about you. And I'd like to know you're going to play this on the level.'

'Give me . . . twenty-four hours.'

'Twenty-four hours,' said the voice obligingly. 'It should be simple, Harry. Just proof that Corder's dead. That's all.'

'And if he isn't? I mean,' said Harry, 'what do you think we're doing out there at his house?'

'Proof that he's dead . . . or else we shall have to come and find *out* what you're doing there.'

There was a click, and the faint background hiss died away.

Thoughtfully Harry moved towards the gate. He was stopped by a bark. A less cheerful bark this time: pretty anguished, in fact. George was jerking at the leash, endeavouring to dislodge the entire bench and bring it along with him.

Harry consulted the blank, uncommunicative windows on all sides. He didn't know if it would do any good to wave, to point at George.

George began to yelp agonizingly. A policeman plodding along the far side of the road gazed suspiciously in.

The sensible thing to do would be to hand George over. And explain how he came to be here?

Harry moaned gently to himself. He untied the lead,

wound its end round his hand, clutched the newspaper parcel and the transistor in his other hand, and departed.

Taxis didn't seem to frequent the south bank of the river. He was halfway back across Waterloo Bridge before one showed up. It took him back to his apartment block behind Curzon Street, and to the Rolls waiting in the basement garage.

He was in no mood to drive straight back. Paul and Caroline ought to be put in the picture, though.

Dropping the package of bisected notes and the radio, still mute, on the divan, and releasing George to sniff inquisitively through the apartment, he went to the phone.

Chino answered. 'They have both left, Mr Rule.'

'Left – where for?'

'They are coming to London. Monsieur Buchet rang for a hire car, and they are on their way now.'

'Why the rush?'

'We had a visitor.'

'Did you, now!'

'He got away, but we have a photograph. The Contessa is going to New Scotland Yard to see if he can be traced.'

'And then?'

'I expect she will come to see if you are in your flat.'

So long as she didn't go gallivanting off on her own, thought Harry. Aloud he said: 'Just what did happen?'

Chino told him, tersely. And added: 'I think they know now that Corder must be dead. So perhaps they will disappear now.'

Like Harry's chances of getting the other half of those fivers. He glanced wryly at the package on the divan. George was working his way past it and on towards the kitchen.

'Looks like we'd better ask Newman to fix a burial. Can't leave Corder lying round like bait for ever.'

He rang off, and went to have a shower. As he was changing, the doorbell throbbed its gentle pulse.

It was Paul.

They sat down and compared notes. The picture they built up confirmed Harry's belief that there would be no further contacts.

'Once your lad gets back and reports, they'll call off operations. Maybe I was called to London just to lower the odds against the break-in boy.'

'Expensive way of doing it.' Paul nodded at the parcel.

'Mm, yes. Maybe, then,' Harry theorized, 'they were doing a two-pronged attack. If one didn't work, the other would.'

Paul Buchet pursed his lips. 'The two approaches were very dissimilar, though. Your man and his radio – that was a nice calculation. Such a flourish to it! An intellectual, I would say, enjoying the gambit. But this other, who hits me on the head, pumps bullets into a coffin, panics, throws things around and runs off ... he is not in the same class.'

'But could be in the same team.'

'Could be,' Paul agreed dubiously. 'Or they could have fallen out – could be playing separate games.'

'One thing's certain,' said Harry. 'All of them, however many there may have been, were scared of Corder. Wherever that loot is stashed away, they wouldn't dare touch it as long as he gave the orders. If they're confident he's dead – if just *one* of them is confident he's dead – then that loot is likely to be collected any time now.'

'We must hope the Contessa gets a positive identification from the police.'

'And contacts us,' said Harry. His gaze wandered to the phone. Their titled colleague had a lamentable tendency to branch out on her own from time to time. 'Maybe I'd better phone Newman.'

He lifted the receiver and began to dial.

Paul got up and idly picked up the package of banknotes. A corner of the newspaper peeled away. He unfolded more of it in order to read a particularly dramatic headline across the front page. Out-of-date newspapers, even when only a few days out of date, are always somehow more fascinating than today's.

Abruptly he said: 'Harry!'

Harry paused in his dialling. Paul was holding the bundle out, the sheet drooping loose. In the top right-hand corner was a pencilled, virtually unreadable scrawl, and a number.

Harry replaced the receiver and held out his hand for the package.

Seen close to, the scribble was still difficult to interpret, but its function was clear enough. It was a newsagent's hasty jotting of an address for the benefit of his delivery boy.

Paul stood by his shoulder. 'Something House? R . . . o . . . p . . . No, that is not an R, is it?'

Harry tore the sheet across and laid it on a table beneath a lamp. He switched on, and stooped over the paper.

'If you'll get me the street guide off that shelf over there – and the guide to business addresses – oh, and while we're at it we may as well have the telephone directories . . .'

In the shallow drawer of the table was a reading glass. Harry scanned it slowly to and fro over the lettering, not so much trying to identify the individual loops and scratches as to see, all at one go, some word that made sense.

'You think that could really be his home address?' said Paul.

'No reason why it shouldn't be.'

'Careless.'

Suddenly a whole syllable shaped itself before his eyes. 'Careless,' he agreed. 'Mistakes always are.'

6

The Contessa said: 'Everything.' She turned the photograph towards Newman. 'Everything you've got on him. If anything. And his address, if you've got it.'

'I'll send down to records.' Newman pressed a buzzer. A uniformed officer came into the room, took the picture, went out. When the door had closed behind him, Newman said amiably: 'Well, now. What happened, Contessa?'

'You asked *us* to handle the case, Inspector. Remember?'

'Meaning you won't tell me.'

'Meaning we prefer to do it our own way.'

Newman's smile stayed fixed on his craggy, pessimistic face. 'Fine. Fine. That's what we're paying you for.'

'We won't be asking for overtime,' Caroline comforted him. 'It shouldn't take long to wrap up now.'

'If we can identify that man.'

'Just so.'

There was a long silence. Newman was no great practitioner in the art of casual conversation. He liked to ask blunt questions and get straight answers; and to give orders and see them carried out. Social chit-chat was beyond him.

After a few minutes the Contessa said: 'It would do no harm to make arrangements for Ralph Corder's funeral. A quiet one, I imagine.'

'With a few sorrowing friends,' said Newman grimly, 'laughing their evil heads off. All right, I'll put it in train.' He couldn't resist asking: 'You think they know all about him now? They know he's dead . . . or . . .?'

The Contessa smiled her most tantalizing smile, and left him guessing.

To their mutual relief the door opened, and the officer returned with the photograph and a police record card. There were two smaller photographs on this, full face and profile.

Newman took them, and deliberately kept the Contessa

waiting while he studied the card. Then he said:

'You're in luck, Contessa. His name's Mason. Alan Mason.'

'And his address?'

'You'll be calling Harry Rule in now, to follow up?' Newman jerked his head towards the phone on his desk. 'Do it from here, if you like. Save time.'

'The address, please,' said the Contessa sweetly.

Newman sighed, and turned the card towards her. She copied the address into her diary, and flicked the tiny silver pencil back into place.

'Thank you, Inspector.'

The drive to Bayswater took longer than she would have wished. She nudged the hired 1300 out of the Victoria congestion only to meet up with a jam caused by a long trailer jack-knifing slowly over a road slippery from a nearby sewer excavation. It took ten minutes to back away and find the side turnings everybody else was searching for.

The street where Mason lived had six parking meters, their spaces all occupied, and 'No Parking' markings everywhere else. She coasted slowly along, counting the ragged terrace of houses up to Number 17; and then had to accelerate as someone on her tail began to sound his horn furiously. She turned left and found herself in a one-way tangle before she could get back and approach the street from another direction.

This time she was lucky. Cars were lined up along one kerb, free of meters or yellow lines. There was just enough space near the corner for her to slide in; and by leaning forward in the driver's seat she could see Mason's front door.

The whole row was probably due for demolition. One end of the street was a pile of rubble, and beyond the wilderness was an upthrust of blocks of flats. Two seedy-looking men stood on one corner arguing. An olive-skinned woman with a string shopping bag brushed close to the 1300 and glanced in. She went on, but looked back, appreciatively, trying for another glimpse of the Contessa's hair and her Balenciaga suit.

If Mason was inside that house, he could stay in all day. Or if he were out, he could stay out all day.

And she could sit here all day. Until some observant policeman asked what she was doing, and how long she proposed to stay – and perhaps got difficult, until she had to get his station to ring the Yard and get her out of the mess, which would give Harry and Paul a great laugh.

The Contessa opened her door and got out.

She was going to do this bit on her own. Do it, pull it off, and present the other two with a dazzling *fait accompli*.

Mason's door remained shut.

She could go along and ring the bell. He would recognize her, but with the advantage of surprise she might simply thrust her way in, scaring him. He seemed to be a man who scared easily.

And then what?

A man crossed the road behind her. It was not until he was on the far pavement that she realized it was Mason. She ducked, and slid back into the car.

He was in a hurry. He almost broke into a run as he went up the short path and the two steps.

The Contessa's long fingers tightened on the wheel.

Mason let himself into the house. And left the door ajar. If he was in a hurry to get in, it looked just as likely that he was in a hurry to get out again.

He was indoors less than a minute. When he reappeared he was carrying a suitcase. He crossed the road; and was out of the Contessa's line of vision.

Her knuckles whitened as she tried to make up her mind. To get out for a better look, to wait, to edge the car round the corner . . .

A car swung across the junction in front of her. She got a good view of Mason's tense profile, almost the same shot as the one on the police card.

She jabbed at the ignition.

Keeping Mason's Vauxhall in sight was a strain. A taxi shouldered its way between them. When she had overtaken that, missing an oncoming bus by inches, she was held up at traffic lights while Mason surged on up a hill.

Fortunately there were other traffic lights; and other taxis and lorries, and cars turning out from intersections across Mason's own path. She caught him up, lost him, and crept up once again as he waited to turn east along the North Circular.

Whatever his destination, it was nowhere in the London area. He kept going, and he was in one hell of a hurry. Beating the lights, accelerating madly through restricted areas, he broke the law along every mile of the way. And to keep him in sight, the Contessa broke it as well.

It would take only one whim of fate and one attentive policeman for her to be run in and for him to get away with it.

She refused to let herself be distracted. All that mattered was to keep him in sight.

Inexorably they headed east. Was he on his way out of the country, with the loot in that case – on his way to Harwich, with everything fixed for him to drive on and then drive off into Denmark or Holland?

In the end, when it came to it, she would have to notify the police.

He was three cars ahead of her in the fast lane of the dual carriageway when she picked up the flash of his left-hand indicator. He swooped into the inner lane before a darkly belching lorry. The Contessa, following suit, found herself driving through the fumes of the lorry's rattling exhaust. She pulled as close to the left as she could go, and could just see that the indicator was still flashing.

There was a turn-off a hundred yards ahead. Mason swung into it, and disappeared round a tight curve. The Contessa turned after him, slowing. It was unlikely that he had picked her up in his mirror – there had been a whole cluster of cars pacing him all the way from London – but in a country lane the situation was a bit different.

It was amazing how quickly the countryside engulfed them. Five minutes from the roar of that dual carriageway, and they were ambling between hedges, through a village of half-timbered and pink-washed cottages.

To her relief a small delivery van came out of a yard

between Mason and herself. Between the hedges, through an occasional gap or just beyond the van, she caught enough glimpses of the Vauxhall to be able to keep a reasonable distance and still know he wasn't drawing away.

A church spire loomed through a patch of trees. Around the clear circuit of a duck-pond the van slowed, and came to a halt before the village store. The Contessa pulled out to pass. The rear number-plate of Mason's car dodged off around yet another twist of the winding lanes.

It wasn't the sort of landscape you'd have associated with Mason. His face, his manner, his whole bearing, and the job he had been involved in – all added up to a city boy. Any idea of him retiring and settling down in a rose-covered cottage just did not ring true.

The Contessa flashed a glance at a tilting signpost and wondered, if she lost Mason now, how she would ever pick him up again.

7

Rearing up against the sky, the office block was a dizzy glitter of glass and concrete. A spark of sunlight struck brightness from a large polished plaque beside the main entrance, listing the companies which occupied this towering palace.

Harry eased the Rolls into a visitor's parking slot across the square from the double doors. He eyed the serried ranks of windows with some concern.

'This is the address all right. Let's hope the paper wasn't from the waiting-room!'

Paul began to get out. 'I'll see what I can find out. If the number on that sheet was a floor, or an internal reference number, we ought to be able to narrow it down.'

He sauntered across the great white flagstones. If there were an even halfway susceptible girl at the reception desk, Paul's lazy charm would get quick results.

Harry drummed his fingers on his knee. He wanted quick results. He was worried – worried, mainly, about the Contessa. She hadn't phoned in; and when he had phoned the Yard just before leaving, it was to learn that she had set out some time ago. Used to working on her own and following her impulses, she was still not entirely settled into the framework of the team. He would have a thing or two to say to her when they met up again. Things about cooperation and not taking unnecessary risks. A frightened prey could turn nasty; could turn and bite.

Paul was returning. He came back across the flags a lot quicker than he had gone.

Harry leaned over to open the passenger door.

'Right,' said Paul. 'Top man. The name's Robard. Reception says he's in his office right at this moment.' He pointed to the parking lot under two great concrete legs of the building. 'That's his car. Second from the right.'

Again Harry leaned forward and raked his gaze up the unrevealing windows. So a man called Robard was sitting somewhere in there. A man whose voice, when he got to hear it, might be the voice he had heard through the transistor radio. A man who might sit there all day, secure in the complacent belief that he was untraceable.

'We go in?' Paul voiced Harry's own thoughts. 'Right into his den?'

'I wouldn't mind having a word with him. Having a word *from* him, I mean.'

Maybe a phone call. Maybe he could speak from the reception desk on some pretext or other, confirm that Robard was who they thought he was, and then play it by ear from there.

'Hold it! Do you think it might be ...?'

A well set-up man with greying hair and an aggressive, almost military walk had come out of the building and was striding towards the line of parked cars.

Harry found himself doing a count-down from the left. Eight ... seven ... six ...

The man reached the second car from the right and stabbed his key into the door on the driver's side.

Harry flicked the ignition of the Rolls.

Before opening the door, the man who must be Robard stood up again and dabbed at his cheek. He took out a handkerchief and dabbed again. A shaft of sunlight through the interstices of the concrete struts cast strange shadows down his cheek. What might have been a bruise stained his left temple, and a trickle of what could have been blood made a lopsided smear.

'Somebody,' Paul confirmed, 'seems to have fallen out with somebody, yes?'

Robard got into his car.

He drove fast but smoothly out into Essex. In pursuit of someone – or trying to get there ahead of someone?

'What I wish to know,' said Paul as the Rolls described a graceful arc round a village duck-pond, 'is what the Contessa is playing at while we are playing at this.'

8

The church stood on a knoll above a winding stream, more than a quarter of a mile from the last cottage in the hamlet to which it supposedly belonged. Its slender flint tower had been patched up sometime in the last couple of centuries with chunks of brickwork looking like red plasticine plugging the cracks; and there were holes in its small, perky spire. A handwritten notice attached to the door of the porch, rusty yellow with rain, listed the Sundays in each month – one a month – when the vicar of the neighbouring parish would conduct a morning service. The grass in the churchyard was long, the gravestones overgrown, a few ornate memorials toppling ominously.

Mason's car turned off the lane on to a bare patch of ground before the lych-gate.

The Contessa, on the curve of the slope above, cut her engine and let the 1300 coast its last few yards into the shelter of a windbreak of elms. Its boot stuck out a few inches into the road, but she did not dare to start the engine again and draw attention to her presence.

She opened the door warily, and let it click half shut.

Birds raised a clamour in the hedgerow. There was the faint, tangy scent of a garden bonfire somewhere down in the hamlet. It was a peaceful scene. But Mason didn't look peaceful as he hurried through the gate and up the weed-clogged path. It was the sort of country churchyard in which Gray might have written his Elegy; but Mason wasn't the type to meditate on an elegy for Ralph Corder.

He vanished into the shadow of the squat south porch.

The Contessa walked down the grass verge of the lane.

The woodwork of the gate was rotten. A dank, sour smell rose from the grass and clumps of mayweed flanking the path. In the porch there was a chill that raised a rash of goose-pimples down her arms.

She stood by the heavily studded oak door, her hand on the rusty ring of the latch.

From within there came a screech that set her teeth on edge. It was as if Mason were dragging his nails along the bottom of some huge metal font.

She risked turning the latch an inch, and pushing inwards.

The door opened an inch.

The noise came again, followed by a heavy thump. The Contessa pushed the door forward and stood back, leaving it to swing in as though on a sudden gust of wind.

There was no response. Nothing but a metallic clink.

She peered in.

The nave was wrapped in gloom. The windows of the north aisle were dark with solemn Victorian stained glass, and although two of the south windows were plain they were shadowed by a close thicket of trees. When something shifted to and fro momentarily in the south aisle, it was hard to tell whether it was some animal trapped in the church or just a slow flicker of shadow.

Caroline moved behind a dusty curtain, half drawn back from what must once have been an enclosure used as a Sunday school.

Where the curtain sagged away from the end of the little chantry she could see, through the gap, Mason hunched over a dark square on the floor of the aisle. He had lifted out a large rectangular memorial tablet and set it against the end of a pew. Beside him was the suitcase, open.

The Contessa kept perfectly still, letting her eyes accustom themselves to the inner twilight of the church.

Mason seemed to pick up two neat handfuls of earth, and turned towards his suitcase.

But they were too neat. There was no spillage, no scattering of soil. He was transferring wads of banknotes from the cache under the floor into his case. Not earth, but money – grubbed up faster and faster, tossed more and more exuberantly into the case. She heard Mason laugh shakily.

And where do we go from here?

The question rang so clearly in her mind that for an instant she was afraid that she had uttered it out loud. But

Mason was still digging, still snickering uncontrollably to himself. She looked back, measuring the distance to the door. Now she regretted not having summoned reinforcements. But if she rushed back to the car now, waited for him, found his eventual destination and so the destination of the money . . .

She turned, and her shoulder brushed the curtain. Its rings clattered against the rail, and as she started away from it her foot caught on the raw edge of a splintered flagstone.

Mason leapt upright and spun towards her.

She would never make the door. No point in trying. She stayed where she was.

'You!' breathed Mason shudderingly.

'Surely you didn't think it would be that easy, Mason?' the Contessa said with more confidence than she felt.

'How do you know my name?'

She shrugged. 'I don't know why that should surprise you. Pretty clumsy behaviour throughout, I'd say. Leaving great big footprints everywhere. If you *will* walk into a trap—'

'A trap?' Mason looked apprehensively around the cold, sombre interior of the church.

'Right at the beginning. Sniffing at the most obvious bait.'

'Corder . . .'

'Corder,' she said, 'was dead all along.'

'Then why was Harry Rule guarding him?'

'With Harry guarding the body, and the police out of sight, we thought you might believe Corder was still alive. We knew he had associates, but we didn't know who they were. And we didn't want them walking off with the money. Which you were too scared to do, weren't you, so long as you thought the big boss was still breathing? You *had* to find out.'

'You're just trying to gain time.'

'How clever of you,' said the Contessa airily. 'But that doesn't alter the facts. You *did* work with Corder on those bank robberies, you *did* come and show yourself near his body – and those *are* the proceeds.' She nodded towards the gaping square in the floor. 'Our operation seems to have been an astounding success.'

'Not for you, it hasn't.'

'You must know I'm not alone here.' She tried to keep it casual enough to be frightening.

'The police?'

'They'll be along. They started the whole thing. They'll just love to wrap it up.'

'We won't wait around to see that.' Mason came past, encircling her and driving her step by step towards the cache of banknotes. 'Put the rest of that money in the case, and we'll be on our way. Move!'

On the edge of the hole the Contessa stood her ground and tried to stare him down.

He said viciously: 'Do as I tell you. That money – get it into the case, and quick about it. Or else.'

His hands hung loosely at his sides. There was no weapon in either of them, but even so he was more than a match for her. And in his present jumpy mood he would be savage and uncontrollable if crossed.

She knelt down and packed the remaining bundles into the case.

'Right. Close it.'

She snapped the catch shut. He wasted no time attempting to replace the stone he had removed, but waved her towards the door.

'You carry the case.'

It was heavy. She made a big business of finding it even heavier, and moving slowly. He crowded her, a few inches to one side, his shoulder jarring into hers. From the corner of her eye she saw his hand dip into his pocket. So he had a gun, after all.

'Tell anybody waiting outside,' he growled, 'that if they make a move you'll be the first one to get it.'

They were a few yards from the porch door when the opening was blocked by a dark shape.

'Mason!'

Mason's breath came out in a shrill, agitated little hiss.

'You,' said the man. 'The Contessa di Contini, I believe?'

'Robard,' whispered Mason. It could hardly have been said to constitute a polite introduction.

Robard, his face still a blur against the light through the porch, said : 'I'll have that case.'

'No!'

'I told you not to make a move without my say-so.'

'And I told *you* I wasn't going to wait forever. I told you—'

'Dear me,' said the Contessa. 'What's that old thing about thieves falling out?'

'The case, please.'

Robard took a step into the church. Mason lurched towards him, his hand groping out of his pocket.

Robard stopped, stood quite still; and fired.

The Contessa heard another shrill of breath from Mason. Tighter, more agonized. And he was no longer there beside her but falling, crumpling.

Robard's gun jutted towards her. His free hand was out, gesturing peremptorily at the case.

She handed it over. He backed away, not taking his eyes off her. He became a silhouette again, and then was blotted out as he slammed the door shut.

The Contessa plunged for the latch.

She opened the door more carefully than he had closed it. Outside, framed in the arch, was a clump of green-encrusted gravestones, bright at one corner with a rash of wild flowers. There was no sign of Robard.

Coming down the hill, resonant against the windbreak of trees on the corner, was a sound she recognized. It was – it had to be – the Rolls.

She edged out into the sunshine.

Robard was racing towards the gate and his waiting car. But the shimmering bulk of the Rolls turned across the lane, and Harry came out before it had even stopped. Behind him was Paul Buchet, sprinting to cut across Robard's path if he made a dash for the meadow over the road.

The gun jerked up.

Harry dived.

The two of them went down. Robard let go of the case,

then made another despairing grab for it. He reared up; went down again as Harry's arm locked round his knees; and this time stayed down.

The Contessa sauntered down the churchyard path and out through the lych-gate.

'Glad you could make it, Harry.'

Harry Rule got to his feet and dusted himself down, knocking away a few rich clods of good Essex earth.

'How many times have I told you not to go chasing off on your own?'

'You sound as bad as Robard.'

'Lucky for you we got on to Robard.'

'Oh, I don't know,' said the Contessa. 'He didn't mean me any personal harm. It was his pal he felt so sore about.'

'His pal?'

'Mason – our elusive visitor.'

'Where is he?'

She waved towards the church door. 'In there. Robard shot him. I don't know how bad he is.'

Paul was lashing Robard's wrists together and loading him unceremoniously into the back of the Rolls. Harry strode towards the church, with the Contessa following at a more leisurely pace.

Inside, he looked along the nave.

'Where?' he demanded.

She edged through the doorway. 'There.' She pointed.

But Mason had gone. There was a dark stain, darker than the damp and the scatterings of earth, a few feet away from a pew end. But no Mason.

'So it wasn't that serious,' said Harry.

'He must have got out while we weren't looking . . .'

There was a smear of blood against the outer arch of the porch. And what might have been another on the grass close to the buttress at the east end. Beyond, the churchyard sloped steeply to a crumbling stone wall, and beyond that was a small field flanked by willows.

'We've lost him,' said Harry furiously.

'But we've got the money. And at any rate one of them. The police should be satisfied with that.'

'*I'm* not satisfied!' he raged. 'I don't like loose ends. Any job we do, I want done properly. I want...'

As they went back to the car, the Contessa resigned herself to a lecture which she had heard, in one form and another, several times before. She said 'Yes, Harry' and 'No, Harry', rather like a bored but dutiful wife, because that was the most painless way of dealing with it.

Then she brightened. She didn't have to drive back with the other two: there was still the hired car, which would have to be returned.

'And when we're on combined ops,' Harry was saying, 'you're not to make a move without my say-so.'

'*Just* like Robard!' she cried, delighted.

9

Inspector Newman was delighted. Paul Buchet was content. The Contessa was happy enough to put her tiny feet up on the tapestry-covered footstool which Harry kicked with an ill grace towards her.

Only Harry Rule was fretful.

'If the police want Mason,' the Countess soothed him, 'it's up to them now. We've established who he is, they know the condition he's in, they ought to be able to pull him in.'

'We ought to have been able to pull him in ourselves.'

There was no arguing with Harry the ultimate professional, Harry the perfectionist.

They sat in his apartment; and she had a nasty feeling that if they sat here long enough he would be making plans to set them all off on a protracted pursuit of the hapless Mason. 'Leave Mason to us,' Newman had said in so many words. But Harry would soon talk himself into taking up where he had left off – and urging the others along with him.

It was time, thought the Contessa, to be going home.

Something cold and wet probed her left leg. She gasped, and sat up.

The dog wagged its tail and nosed her other leg.

'What are we going to do about George?' she asked.

'George?' Harry looked down. 'I don't know,' he said vaguely.

'He can't stay here.'

'Why not?'

'You'd let the poor little thing starve. You'd forget him for days on end.'

'I'd do no such thing.'

'Can you honestly promise,' she challenged, 'to take George for a long walk in the park every day?'

'Er—'

'Can you?'

'It's not exactly my scene,' Harry admitted.

'Exactly. I mean, exactly it's not. So I think I'd better take him to Rome with me. Why don't you come too?'

'I've got work to do,' said Harry sourly.

'Or to Paris with me?' Paul suggested.

The telephone jangled into life. Harry reached for the receiver.

'Rule. Yes. Look – how did you get my number? Who? Oh, he did.' Harry shrugged. 'All right. Yes.'

The Contessa leaned back and reached for her drink.

'Put him on,' Harry said. Then: 'Sir Walter. Yes, Rule here. Yes, I do remember. So does my colleague, Paul Buchet, I fancy.'

Paul raised a questioning eyebrow.

Harry was nodding. Then frowning. Then he was saying: 'She's down in Spain? I don't think I can get there for a week or two. Something I have to clear up here, first.' A voice crackled in the receiver. 'Quite,' said Harry. 'A bit of a delicate situation, hm? Sir Walter . . . leave it to me, and the moment I can see my way to doing something about it I'll let you know. No, of course I won't. Could be within a week. Two weeks, maybe.'

He put the receiver down. Paul's eyebrow continued its query. The Contessa looked at Harry over her glass.

He said: 'Sir Walter Crediton.'

'Ah, yes.' Paul remembered. 'We debugged two of his factories when he had that spot of bother with sabotage.'

'This time it's his daughter.'

'She needs debugging?'

'She's in danger in Spain. Or so he thinks. He'd like me to make some judicious enquiries, without getting her mad.'

'Sir Galahad Rule now,' the Contessa observed.

'Danger?' said Paul.

'Moral danger. On the Costa Brava.'

'Who *isn't* in moral danger on the Costa Brava?'

'He sounds to me like the usual fussy father,' said Harry. 'Daughter's a spoilt brat, rebelling against parental authority – come home and all will be forgiven. That sort of thing.'

'Hardly our sort of thing, though.'

'No. I don't mind helping out; but it'll have to wait. One thing at a time,' said Harry puritanically. 'And first things first.'

Meaning Mason, thought the Contessa.

She said: 'Rome for me.'

'Paris for me,' said Paul.

They both looked at Harry, offering him a last chance to relax.

'I'm staying right here,' he said.

They sighed, and left him to it.

Part Two

DISAPPEARING TRICK

I

The hotel had a faded elegance which set it apart from its brasher neighbours around the Place de l'Etoile. Faded, but not by any means shabby: elegant with a cool nostalgia which attracted older people, and some not-so-old people who preferred to avoid familiar faces – and inquisitive faces. In its discreet, unruffled lobby the turmoil of the Paris traffic was subdued, like the voices of the staff, to a deferential murmur. It was a haven in which to meditate and to get one's bearings again.

Harry Rule stood by the newspaper rack, sunk in contemplation of the folded front page of *Le Monde.* He hardly turned his head when an elderly lady emerged from the door marked *Mesdames*; but Paul Buchet, reading a magazine in an armchair beneath a potted palm, would not have been unaware of the stiffening of his fingers and a new tension in his shoulder blades.

The woman's face was concealed behind a veil. She leaned on a stick, and tapped her way towards the revolving doors. At a brief nod of her head, a porter lifted two bags which had been set beside the reception desk.

A commissionaire in a uniform worthy of the *Grande Armée* stepped forward.

And the Contessa di Contini came out of the same door as the elderly lady. She jerked her head once at Paul, once at Harry.

Paul folded the magazine and got up.

Harry spun smartly on his heel and went after the frail, gentle old creature. For someone so frail she had remarkably wide shoulders.

He tapped her on one of them.

She reacted more sharply than one might have expected, raising her left hand as she turned. Deftly Harry flicked up the edge of her veil, smiled with satisfaction at what he saw; and delivered a swift upper cut to the jaw.

The stick flew one way, her purse the other. She went down. The purse slithered along the floor and came to rest against the horrified manager's right shoe. As the catch snapped open, a shiny automatic peeped coyly out.

The tranquillity of the lobby was shattered. A woman in one corner began to squeal '*A l'assassin, à l'assassin*', the commissionaire bellowed something, the porter dropped both bags with a resounding thud. The manager waved frantically towards the desk and yelled for the girl there to call the police.

Harry took out his wallet, opening it to show his detective's shield. 'I'm the police. Kind of.'

'*Mais, c'est affreux ... c'est ...*'

'It is, isn't it?'

Paul stood over the woman as she began to scramble to her feet with remarkable lack of feminine dignity. The Contessa closed in from the other side.

'But do please call the cops,' Harry went on. 'Their opposite numbers in London will be only too glad to hear the news.'

'*Mais, m'sieur* ... sir, please ... to hit an old lady ...'

'Old lady?' said Harry sceptically.

He stooped, and as Paul wrenched her round to face him he grabbed the veil and twisted both veil and hat upwards.

Mason glared back at him.

'So glad we could make it,' said Harry. 'He's just the way you described him, Caroline. Only worse.'

'How?' rasped Mason, trying to wrench free from Paul's steely grip and then giving it up. 'How'd you find me?'

'We have a nose for that kind of thing.'

'But I didn't leave any tracks. I covered all my traces.'

'Not from us,' said Harry. 'Nobody disappears from us. But nobody!'

2

The headlines were not much to Harry's taste. They had kept the whole business secret and unfussy until now. But when you unmasked a sweet old dowager in the well-frequented lobby of a leading Paris hotel and shipped her back to London as a wanted criminal – with a stubble of beard and without the mauve hat and veil – you were bound to attract attention. One of the more lurid Paris weekend papers splashed a big feature on the activities of the Protectors. Other papers in other countries copied. It was free advertising; but the Protectors could manage without that.

'Now are you satisfied?' asked Paul on the Sunday evening, entertaining them on the balcony of his fourth-floor apartment.

'Dragging me all the way here from Rome just for a thirty-second showdown!' lamented the Contessa.

'I thought you'd want to be in at the kill. Besides, I had to be sure . . . um . . .'

'Sure that the lady was a gent? There must have been an easier way of finding out. Or surely you could have hired one of Paul's girl friends to go into the loo. It's the most expensive penny *I've* ever spent.'

'I like us all to play our part,' said Harry, leaning back luxuriously.

'And now,' said the Contessa, 'will you relax? Just for a few days – please?'

Harry grinned at her. She was really rather delectable. Now that they had wrapped up this last bit of the job, he could see her as a human being rather than part of their own special machine. A very beautiful human being. Warm, witty, and most decorative. Good company – with no strain, no strings. There would never again be anybody for her, not after her husband. He had met Luigi, long ago; and didn't blame her. But it made her easy to be with. So much easier than any restless woman with an urge to tease, provoke, demand a response.

He said: 'I'll take you for a long, health-giving walk tomorrow.'

'You won't. You'll take me for a short, easy-going stroll.'

'It's a deal.'

In the morning they did just that, sauntering along the banks of the Seine, watching the barges, talking idly when they felt like it and remaining companionably silent when it suited them. It was not until close on lunch-time that Harry began to fret. He couldn't understand his own unease at first. Then he identified the symptoms. Somebody was watching him. Even before he could pick anyone out from the crowds, or from the casual groups above the water, along the bookstalls, leaning over the bridges, he knew there was somebody there; could feel the gaze boring into the back of his neck.

Abruptly the Contessa said: 'Harry, you're at it again.'

'At what?'

'I don't know. Something. Why don't you relax? Even a watch spring runs down occasionally, you know.'

'Not if you wind it regularly.'

'You're just a twenty-four-hour surveillance man. You know that?'

'I'm a professional,' said Harry.

'Meaning that I'm just a talented amateur.'

'I didn't say that.'

'But you often think it, don't you? You think that where you work, I play.' When he refused to answer, she said: 'Well, at least you don't dispute the word "talented".'

'You're pretty good.'

'Making allowances for my sex?'

'Making allowances for your sex,' he conceded.

They crossed into Montmartre and began to climb. There was a bistro a few yards from the second turning. Or had been when he was last here. He had been looking forward to the prospect of the food they dished out there – looking forward to it from the moment they started out. Yet now his appetite was failing. He was on edge, querulous.

They hadn't said a word since they began to climb. The Contessa, who had obviously been doing her own line in brooding, burst out suddenly: 'You don't *have* to make allowances for me. I won't have it. I'll stand or fall on results!'

'OK. Then answer me something. Who's the guy who's been following us ever since we left Paul's place?'

She stumbled on the ragged edge of the sidewalk, and looked back down the narrow street. It was empty.

'I don't see anyone.'

'He's good.'

'Stop putting on an act. There isn't anyone there, and there hasn't been all morning.'

'Takes a professional to spot him,' said Harry.

'Why, you—'

'Tell me something else. Where precisely are we?'

'In the *rue de la . . . des . . .*'

'Quite so. And where's the car?'

'Where we left it, I hope.'

'Just round the next corner, to be precise,' said Harry. 'We started twenty yards from here, and we've come full circle. But you didn't notice, did you?'

'You're insufferable.'

'Sense of direction – that's important, too. Can be vital, in some circumstances.'

Fuming, the Contessa cast a hostile glance down the side street as they passed. The Citroen sat in the shade of the tall, shuttered house where they had left it.

Harry caught her arm, quickened their pace, and led her into the dusky interior of a café on the far side of the road. A young couple sat in the most secluded corner, their elbows on the table, staring into each other's eyes. The *patron* was propping up the end of the bar. He came round it as Harry pulled out a chair from the table in the window, and the Contessa sat down.

Two central segments of the window were opened inwards like square glass doors, to admit some fresh air – though the air in fact was hot and stale, tinged with onions and petrol and an echo of some street-cleaning chemical.

Two glasses of red wine were set down on the table. At the same moment a sandy-haired man with a fawn lightweight jacket stopped on the pavement outside, looking up and down the precipitous street.

Harry put his head in the opening and said gently : '*Bonjour.*'

The man spun round. He was young, with freckles spraying out from the bridge of his nose, and oddly pale, wide grey eyes. He grinned awkwardly.

'You spotted me.' The inflection was American. He ambled away from the window and came up the two steps into the café, signalling for a third glass. 'I was hoping you would.'

'Hoping?' echoed the Contessa.

'Well, I wouldn't want to hire somebody who didn't know his job. Or her job.' He sat down. When the glass of wine had been set before him, he raised it in a silent toast, drank, and introduced himself. 'Huron. Brad Huron.'

Harry emitted a dry whistle. 'Carl Huron?'

'Is my dad.'

Harry had come across many references to the shipping millionaire at one time and another, in newspapers and magazines. Sometimes he had featured in stories of adventurous expansion, putting more than one shipyard back on its feet with huge orders. There had been other stories – about ruthless takeover bids, elimination of competitors, and massive bribery to evade Customs and other regulations. Columnists had spread themselves on his three marriages and three divorces. But Harry could recall no reference to a son.

The Contessa said : 'What was that about hiring us?'

'I can afford it. Don't you worry about that.'

'We're not worrying about that,' said Harry levelly. 'Not yet.' Inexplicably, the unease which had been pricking at him all morning had intensified now that their tracker had shown himself. He was a bright, fresh-faced young man with an engaging, artless voice; but Harry wasn't happy. He said : 'First we need to know just what it is you want.'

'Sure,' said Brad Huron. 'I want you to disappear me.'

'To do what?'

'The vanishing trick. Whisk me off into thin air.'

'Take it nice and slow and easy.'

Brad Huron said: 'I got to reading about that stunt of yours the other day. Pouncing on that guy who was making out with the old woman act. And it wasn't the first time, was it?'

Harry shrugged modestly.

'Wouldn't mind betting you were tied in with that case a year or two back – Johnny Quick, the quick-change hoodlum . . . swapping identities a dozen times, and then he got rounded up.'

'It's not so easy to get away nowadays,' said Harry. 'To drop out of sight. Become somebody else. News travels too fast. Communications, air travel, teleprinters and data banks – they've shrunk the world. Aren't many places left to hide in.'

'That's what Malloy said.'

'Malloy?'

'My . . . friend. Good old Malloy.' Brad barked a short laugh at some private joke. 'I said to him, these guys do it all wrong. There must be a way. And he said pretty well what you just said – the world's gotten too small. There's no place to go. So I bet him.'

'That you could do it better?'

'Right!'

'How much did you bet?' asked the Contessa, fascinated.

'Ten thousand bucks.'

'Ten thou . . .'

'To disappear,' laughed Brad. 'Forever. You get the picture?'

Harry was certainly beginning to get a picture. It wasn't a comfortable one. Whatever was wrong, it was something very wrong indeed. Again he wondered why he had never heard of Carl Huron having a son, when the tabloids had carried pretty nearly everything else about Huron and his empire. And wondered, baffled, what kind of con game this pretender – if he was a pretender – could be formulating.

'You know us madly rich, gay young things,' Brad was

mockingly addressing himself to the Contessa. 'I made this bet—'

'To disappear forever?' said Harry.

Something in his tone must have warned the young man. There was a slight hesitation, then he said: 'Well ... let's say a week. A month, maybe. Until I've proved my point.'

The Contessa turned her glass between her fingers. 'But why us?'

'Because we're detectives,' Harry contributed. 'We find people. We know the mistakes they make. So we know what not to do.'

'Say, you're fast. I knew I'd made the right choice. Knew it as soon as I read about you. Why, I'll bet you're the best disappearers in the business. We could all get one hell of a kick out of this.' He looked from Harry to the Contessa, and back again. 'Well, what do you say?'

No, said a loud firm voice inside Harry's head. That's what he was going to say: No. But not outright, not too bluntly. Before committing himself he had to stall, had to make a few enquiries – discreet but fast.

'Sounds as though it might be fun,' ventured the Contessa. When he didn't respond, she said: 'Oh, come on, Harry. What's the matter? Isn't it *professional* enough for you?'

Harry began to get to his feet. 'We'll talk about it.'

'But I want to be disappeared right now,' Brad Huron protested. 'Today!'

'We'll talk about it,' said Harry harshly, 'back at Buchet's place.'

He tried to signal a warning to the Contessa, but she refused to acknowledge his gaze. Then, as if in tacit surrender, she said: 'Oh, all right. My car's just across the street, Mr Huron. Harry – you'll settle?'

Harry turned towards the counter. As he was fishing for change, the click of the Contessa's heels quickened on the cobbles outside. All at once he knew what had been going on behind that suave mask of hers.

He spilled coins across the metal surface, and turned to run.

As he reached the corner of the side street the Citroen roared into life and came out, sliding over the uneven road, righting itself, and then rocking away down the slope like a car gone crazy on a roller-coaster.

3

They joined the mainstream of traffic down a long boulevard. The Contessa sat tense when they slowed in a huddle of cars blocking one entrance to a square, and looked a dozen times in her driving mirror. Then they disentangled themselves, and moved on, and she sat back and let her hands rest more lightly, more confidently on the wheel.

'Lesson One in disappearing,' she said: 'don't talk – move!'

And to herself she added silently and derisively: Talented amateur . . . !

Brad Huron was glancing doubtfully at her. He, too, might see her in that light. It was Harry Rule he had been after in the first place: Harry he had wanted for the job. Well, she was going to show both of them a thing or two. If spoilt, wealthy young Mr Huron thought it would be funny to disappear, then disappear he should – not only from his friend but from the ace pursuer of them all, from Harry Rule himself.

She said: 'How long have we got?' He seemed dazed, perhaps by the speed of their departure. 'How long,' she asked, 'before he starts looking?'

'Mm?'

'Whoever you made the bet with. He'll come looking for you, won't he?'

'Oh, yeah. Sure.' His lips worked. He was more than ever like a spoilt kid; a peevish kid who had fallen out with a friend and was determined to make a monkey out of that friend. 'Sure they'll come looking,' he said.

She took a short cut through back streets which even Paul Buchet would have found it hard to identify, and headed for St Germain.

'You really think you can do it?' said Brad. 'Completely disappear me?'

'Stake my life on it.'

He chuckled. There was something unpremeditated, explosive in it. The Contessa glanced sharply at him; but he was relaxing now, watching the tall houses flash by, studying their balconies and window-boxes as blissfully as any tourist on a conducted tour.

Only when they turned sharp right and tilted down into momentary darkness did he blink, and mutter a protest.

'Leave it to me,' the Contessa murmured.

The Citroen purred smoothly down the ramp into the underground car park. Strip lights picked out the glossy colours of a Simca, a Renault and a bright new yellow Porsche.

She backed into a slot beside the Porsche and indicated that her passenger should get out.

'This one, I think.'

He stood by the gleaming yellow flank of the Porsche and patted it. 'We gonna steal a car now?' He almost giggled with delight.

'Who said steal? They're all mine.'

A question, maybe a whole string of questions, trembled on his lips. The Contessa was in no mood to deal with them. She was making it all up as she went along, and she didn't want to have to explain each and every move. First this substitute car, and then what? New clothes for Brad, of course. And just for the fun of it, why not take a leaf out of Mason's book? Harry would appreciate the joke later, when it was all over and she had proved what she could do, single-handed.

She laughed.

'What's so funny?' Brad demanded.

She gave him another silent command, a jerk of the thumb towards the passenger seat. She slid in behind the wheel, and the Porsche hummed into life and went off up the ramp, out into the sunshine.

The Contessa sketched a long arc round the west of the city, then swung in towards the centre until she found what she was looking for – a wide square with a sprawling, chaotic market.

She left Brad in the car while she went shopping.

4

'Ran out on you?' Paul put his head back and laughed. A lot more exuberantly than was called for, in Harry's view. 'Oh, this is going to be interesting.'

'Not the way I see it.'

'Oh, come on, Harry. She was a step ahead of you, that's all. Admit it. It was very neat.'

'Maybe.'

'What's eating you?'

'Something about that Huron guy I didn't trust.'

'And while you were being over-cautious about the job, Caroline took it – and carted him off.' Paul shook his head admiringly.

Harry stood by the window of Paul's apartment, his hands thrust into his pockets, his head sunk. Somewhere out there, in that tumultuous world which was Paris, the Contessa was probably laughing just the way Paul was laughing. Or maybe was driving out into the woods, out along the Seine valley, out in any direction that took her fancy.

He hoped for her sake that it would continue to be a laugh.

'Let's see how she makes out,' Paul was saying behind him. 'And don't snap her head off when she gets back, Harry.'

Was there really such a person as Brad Huron?

The telephone rang. Paul picked up the receiver. 'Buchet. *Oui, le même. Oui, je . . .*' Then he was speaking English again; and the gaiety had gone out of his voice. 'Huron? Yes, we *do* know something about . . .'

Someone was grating out words furiously at the other end. Paul's face darkened. Finally he said:

'I think you'd better send someone over. Yes, that's right. You've got it.'

The hackles on Harry's neck had been rising. He felt

danger, smelt it – full strength now, no longer a fidgety suspicion.

He said : 'All right, let's have it.'

'Carl Huron,' said Paul. 'He's in Paris. Has his headquarters here nowadays, it seems. And he seems to be . . . worried.'

'About his son?'

'Something about a newspaper cutting, and a man called Malloy, and an escape.'

'Whose escape?'

'His son's.' Paul spoke in little more than a whisper. 'Someone's on his way over to see us.'

The someone was Carl Huron himself, accompanied by a brawny man with a pugilist's battered nose and large, powerful hands which made futile, twitchy little gestures whenever Huron raised his voice.

And Huron raised his voice in fits and starts of rage.

He was a steely-haired man with implacable eyes and a jaw like an ice-breaker. He had been accustomed all his life to men jumping when he spoke – jumping into action, or jumping with fear.

His opening snarl was : 'My son *did* contact you, then, Rule?'

'We met him, yes.'

'Then where is he now?'

'You sound very concerned,' said Harry tightly.

'Look, Rule, do you have any idea—'

'No ideas whatsoever,' said Harry. 'Maybe you can supply a few.'

'I want to know where that boy is.'

Paul intervened quickly. 'Harry, remember our ethics. This gentleman might be in league with whoever's chasing Brad Huron – whoever he made the bet with.'

Carl Huron said : 'The man he made the bet with is in hospital with a compound fracture of the skull.'

'And your son—'

'My son put him there.'

Harry was conscious of a sickening surge and plunge in

his stomach. He forced himself to keep it calm, to fight down the level of Huron's own rage. He said stolidly:

'I think you'd better tell us the lot.'

'Brad isn't normal.' Huron, too, was having to force things – forcing himself to tell what he had kept secret from the world for a long time . . . for his son's lifetime. 'Never has been. He's deranged. Homicidal.'

'Homicidal, and walking about loose?'

The man at Huron's side flinched as the shipping magnate turned to glare at him. 'Walters here,' rasped Huron, 'and a man called Malloy were supposed to be looking after him. The two of them, plus four guards on rota, and with dogs and a twelve-foot fence to help them. A fence right round a very special, very specially constructed villa way out near Fontainebleau. And still he got out!'

'We . . . I guess we got slack,' mumbled Walters. 'He hadn't given any trouble in months. And especially these last few weeks, he seemed so . . . well, lucid.'

'Lucid?' growled Huron. 'Lucid enough to make a bet with Malloy, after reading all that stuff in the papers – and then lucid enough to batter Malloy over the head before starting out.'

Walters looked at Harry Rule. 'And he's armed,' he said. 'He's got a forty-four automatic and three clips of ammo.'

Harry brushed past the two of them and made for the phone.

'What are you doing?' Huron demanded.

'Calling the police.'

'But I won't have that. I've always handled this myself.'

'Not any more.'

'They'll put him away . . . commit him. Whatever he is,' said Huron, his voice splintering, 'he's still my son.'

'Yes,' said Harry. 'And he's with our Contessa.'

The big man crumpled, ever so slightly, in on himself. Walters gave him a covert glance, as though waiting for an instruction to knock Harry Rule away from the phone.

But Harry put the call through. Out went the full alert. He ought to have felt some sense of relief; felt that something was being done, and it was going to be all right. He felt no such thing.

'What can I do now?' asked Carl Huron wearily, a beaten man.

'Go home.' Harry sensed the years of misery that must have lain behind all this. The anguish which might have done much to make Huron the financial success he undoubtedly was, driven to forget his personal tragedy by savage application to work and work and more work. 'Wait,' he said, with a touch of sympathy. 'Stay by the phone.'

'Yes.' Huron turned towards the door, then stopped. 'Mr Rule . . . when they find my son . . .'

'They know he's a sick man.'

There was a long, long minute after the door had closed behind Huron and Walters before Paul said unsteadily:

'The police won't find Caroline.'

'Not if she doesn't want to be found.'

'We can't just sit here. Not like that poor wretch Huron, just sitting and waiting.'

'That little squirt you used last year – the little know-all – what was his name?'

'Leprave?'

'That's the one. Have him contact every stoolie in town. She's going to have to dump that car soon. I want to know where.'

It took less time than he had expected. But it wasn't exactly good news. In any other circumstances they might have laughed. But it was no time for laughter.

Paul, at the phone as Leprave reported in, said: 'She dumped the car all right.'

'Where?'

'In town. In her own garage!'

A typical gesture, when they came to think of it. The Contessa thumbing her nose at pursuers. But she was taking it for granted that any pursuers would be a scatterbrained friend or two of a poor little rich boy. She didn't know what was really riding beside her.

Harry said: 'So she took another car. Does he know which one?'

Paul snapped a question; listened; and said: 'A yellow Porsche.'

'The number . . .?'

At last he began to feel the tingle which always came when action was possible. Not just speculation, but real action. No guarantee of results – of the right results, anyway – but at least a sporting chance.

Harry Rule never asked for more than just that chance.

By late afternoon his Mustang had found its way to a café on the edge of the market-place. The stalls were being cleared: the secondhand clothes packed away, the fruit and vegetables being sold off for what they would fetch. A few trucks nudged their way over the cobbles. Two old women with black shawls swept the gutters; and another woman looking like a third triplet picked over the shreds of material and discarded boxes in the hope of discovering some neglected treasure.

'Un café, m'sieur . . . du vin . . .?'

Harry pushed hair back from his damp brow. The day had been close and oppressive. Now it felt like thunder; and for himself, he was blowing up a storm. He said:

'Information. I'm looking for a woman. Tall, slim, beautiful.'

The owner of the café smiled. 'Who is not, *m'sieur*?'

'This one has an odd sort of left eyebrow. Out of tune with the right, if you know what I mean. Looks like she's always laughing at you – or with you. Green and hazel and . . .'

Hell, how could you describe Caroline's mocking, ever-changing eyes?

'Now that I think I may have seen. Yes.'

'With a man,' said Harry eagerly. 'American. Chunky. Friendly face.'

'Alas, no. That is not it.'

'You've seen no-one? No-one like that?'

'A beautiful woman, yes. The way you describe her, almost. Earlier this afternoon. But she was not with a man. With her mother.' He shrugged, spread his hands apologetically. 'Not a man, *m'sieur*. Just an old lady.'

Harry nodded absently and turned away. Then it struck him.

'An old lady?'

'Oui.'

'But you didn't see her face, eh?'

'I must think. Please, I do not remember, it is a busy day, there are many people, I—'

'She was veiled,' said Harry flatly.

'Pardon?'

'She wore a veil.' Harry made fluttering motions in front of his face.

'Ah, yes. So. *Oui, c'est vrai. Parfaitement.*'

'Where did they go?'

'Across the square to an auto. And then, I do not know. They drive off. Towards Paris, I think. It was . . . ah' – he struggled for words – *'très jaune.'*

'A yellow Porsche?'

'C'est bien cela.'

So far so good. And yet not so good, when you came to add it up. The Contessa had dressed her client as an old woman, as though inviting their pursuers to share her perverse sense of humour – almost, derisively, to draw attention to them. But where were the two of them heading? Back into Paris, the man implied. That must surely have been a blind. Or simply the easiest way of getting out of the crowded square.

Harry went to the door of the café, studied the general flow of the traffic, and beckoned to Paul to leave the Mustang and come inside. When he had telephoned the police with added details of the veiled old lady who would now be sitting beside the Contessa, he went to the table where Paul had set up two glasses of Pernod.

'I expected better,' he said critically.

'The brand of whisky you get in a place like this—'

'I meant the Contessa. I expected something a lot better from her.' He drank, and felt the backs of his teeth fur up. 'A straight steal from that lout Mason – it's pretty crude!'

'However, it worked,' Paul pointed out. 'Left us with eggs on our head.'

'Face,' said Harry abstractedly.

'Eh?'

'Face. The vernacular is "egg on your face".' He drummed with his fingers on the table; and stopped on a downbeat. 'Just a minute. *Just* a minute! I'm right.'

'You are?' said Paul sardonically.

'The Contessa. Sure she can do better than that. She's *doing* better right now.'

'I do not follow.'

'Dressing him as an old lady!' Harry drained his glass, coughed, and stood up. 'Sure it's corny. And obvious. And the car, too – why a Porsche? A bright yellow Porsche, when she could have had her pick of half-a-dozen cars. She's blazing a trail a myopic boy scout could follow!'

Paul caught on. 'She's going to switch – to switch completely.'

'Right.'

'But to what?'

'Put yourself in her shoes. What would you do?'

'Get another car.'

'Which car? You don't want to hire one. That takes time, needs papers . . . questions, delays, just one little slip and you give yourself away. Taxis are out: they can be traced too easily. You need a car that's cool. A car nobody is looking for any more . . . because they already found it.'

They were back into the Mustang within a matter of seconds. Harry skidded round a pile of bashed-in cardboard boxes, avoided an old woman who stepped off the kerb near his wing and remained in the gutter, obviously prepared to go on cursing him until he was far out of sight, and headed in towards the centre of the city once more.

Not too far in, though. He knew the route to the Contessa's apartment block well enough. Knew the drive-in to the underground garage. And was sure he knew, now, which cars would be in which slots.

And which one would be missing.

They halted under the sallow glow of the strip lighting and looked along the gleaming rank of multi-coloured bonnets.

The yellow Porsche was brightest of all.

Harry slid out from behind the wheel and went to it. The offside door wasn't locked. He opened it, and an old-fashioned bombazine dress fell from the seat to the floor of the garage. Still on the seat were a coat, a hat and a veil.

'Square one!' said Harry.

His voice boomed faintly back at him across the cavern of the garage. Next to the Porsche was a gap. A quick appraisal confirmed what had been taken from it.

The Citroen was out on the roads again.

5

Brad Huron said : 'What are we waiting about for? Let's be on our way.'

He lacked the Contessa's ability to conserve her energies, to sit as relaxed yet as watchful as a cat.

The Citroen was parked in a cul-de-sac opening off a crescent of dusty trees and neglected flower-beds. Flowering shrubs which needed cutting back provided a useful screen, through a gap in which the Contessa could just see one entrance to the square and the steps up to the *arrondissement* police station.

'Lesson Two in disappearing,' she explained. 'Stop running. And get a good look at who's chasing you.'

'Yeah, but what's stopping them getting a good look at *us*?'

'They won't expect us to be still hanging about in this neighbourhood.'

'I hope you know what you're doing.' His voice was a petulant rasp. 'I've got a lot at stake.'

'So have I.'

More than you might imagine, the Contessa added to herself. She thought of the homage she was determined to exact from Harry Rule when she had fulfilled the terms of this contract. He was going to eat humble pie. Once this was over he was going to show her a lot more respect.

The Porsche had been displayed in that market square for all to see. In the café and the market-place she had drawn as much attention as possible to Brad and herself. More than one witness could report that she had arrived with a meaty young American, and within a short time had been seen in the company of an oddly dressed old lady with big feet and hands and a gawkily unfeminine walk. The stallholder who had sold her the clothes could be traced, and would talk. The man in the café would talk. By now the sum would be adding up. Whoever Brad's betting friend set on the trail would soon be in full pursuit of a yellow Porsche with an old woman and a younger woman in it.

Even before leaving the square to dump the Porsche she had seen a familiar face. Somebody knew his stuff all right. Hiring Leprave was the first thing to do when you were in a hurry to track someone down. Seedy little Leprave was the fastest ferret in the business.

But not the kind to handle a whole assignment on his own. There had to be somebody behind him to give the orders and collate the facts.

'If your friend shows up,' she said : 'you know . . . what's his name . . .?'

Brad fidgeted and stared resentfully at her.

'The friend who made the bet,' she prompted.

'Oh, him. Malloy.'

'If you see him heaving into view—'

'Malloy won't be coming,' said Brad.

'You sound very sure of that.'

'Not him.' Brad grinned a weird, slanting grin. 'Not Malloy.'

'Then whoever he takes on to do the chasing for him—'

'Spain,' said Brad curtly, out of the blue. 'Let's get out of here. I want to disappear in Spain. That's what I want.'

'Spain? But . . .'

She stopped; and hunched forward, peering at a car drawing up before the *poste de police*.

'What's wrong?'

'The man you made a bet with,' said the Contessa. 'He's played an ace.'

'Cut out the riddles.'

'He's hired Harry Rule to find us.'

She watched Harry leave the Mustang and go into the station. His last few steps were obscured by strands of a straggling bush.

Now she would comply with Brad's wishes, and get moving. And move fast and clever. After all, Harry was a professional – the greatest – wasn't that pretty well what he had boasted to her?

It added a whole new savour. Herself against Harry. And both of them getting paid in the end. Good for the organization's funds! And for sharpening their wits.

She really had to show Harry something. Including a clean pair of heels.

The Citroen edged out of the cul-de-sac and along the crescent to a junction some distance from the market square. Then they turned south.

'Spain,' Brad repeated.

'Honestly, we'd do better to stay in Paris. It's easier to hide right on the doorstep than—'

'I aim to get right away from here. All right, so it's up to you to get me clear, and disappear me. I leave it to you. But not right here. A long, long way away from them.'

'From *them*?'

'Greenland, if you like,' he cried.

The Contessa shivered. 'All right. Spain it is.'

It was dusk as they cleared Paris – a lingering, violet dusk which softened the jagged edges of the receding suburbs and seemed, at last, to have some softening effect on Brad as well.

Reminiscently he said: 'That sure was strange, that business of those clothes.'

'You didn't fancy yourself as a dear old dowager?'

'I never knew women's clothes were so . . . well, technical. All those hooks and straps and stuff.'

'You mean it was all a surprise to you?'

'Sure.'

'And that's a surprise, too. To me.'

'Huh?'

'Women's clothes being so . . . "technical".' The Contessa laughed, inviting him to share the laugh. 'Don't you have any girl friends?'

'Dad forbid it.'

'Forbid it?' She noticed that he was looking away from her, out of the window, as though regretting having let that slip. 'But you must be . . .' She tried to keep it flippant, the way she'd tried it in the first place. 'You're over twenty-one.'

'Thirty,' he said.

She wouldn't have given him that many years. His face was strangely innocent and unlined. Maybe his father's wealth had protected him from experience, from reality, from having to work and worry. It would explain his naivety – but not, she thought uneasily, his flickering bouts of barely controlled fury. A spoilt child ... and an unpredictable one.

As far as Orléans she stayed on the main highway, but then branched off on to quieter side roads. It was too easy to be spotted on the main road. Or was it? She switched on her headlights, picking out the corner of a ragged barn and then a street of single-storey houses, leaning towards the road and then fleeing away behind. Perhaps their progress was more noticeable along these narrow by-ways.

With a bit of luck the pursuit would still be concentrated on the Porsche. But now that Harry was involved, she wasn't too sure about that. Harry knew her too well. He might out-guess her. In which case she would have to keep guessing one ahead of him.

She began to hum to herself.

Brad found the sound reassuring. He said: 'We're in the clear.'

'I think so.'

'Then I've done it.' He watched the swathe of light ahead, slicing along a line of poplars. 'Disappeared. Nobody knows where I am.'

'Nobody,' said the Contessa. 'Except me.'

His head came slowly round. She was aware that he was looking at her; but the road began to wind tortuously, and she couldn't take her eyes off the road to see what his expression might be.

As darkness settled over the countryside she said: 'We don't want to keep on all night.'

'Oh, yes we do.'

She persuaded herself that the note of menace in his voice was an exaggerated joke. 'Not right into Spain,' she said.

'Right into Spain.'

'I know a little inn near the border. Maybe we could get

breakfast there. Or pull off towards the coast before then, take it a bit easier—'

'We keep straight on,' said Brad. 'That's the way I want it.'

'Real French cooking,' she coaxed. 'All around us. A bottle of wine. This is a holiday, Brad – isn't that the way you want it?'

He remained silent. It was not until they had roared through another drowsy village, frightening a cluster of chickens holding an evening discussion on the verge of the road, that he said more easily:

'Sure. Just so long as we don't let anyone sneak up on us.'

They had been going for another hour when she saw the intermittent flicker of the pink light warning that the fuel tank was down to its last two gallons.

'We'll need a filling station pretty soon.'

Brad, she was discovering, wasn't an easy passenger to have along. The mere mention of a filling station tensed him up again, and she could almost feel the aching tautness of his muscles as, thankfully, she saw pump lights ahead and slowed on to the forecourt.

The engine died. There was silence.

She wound down the window and waited for an attendant to appear out of the long, rickety shack which appeared to be a home at one end and a repair bay at the other.

A faint breeze whispered off a distant hillside.

'Pretty lonely out there,' observed Brad.

She thought of the road ahead. 'It gets lonelier.'

'That's good. Very good.'

Another faint, uneven sound added itself to the sighing of the breeze. Somewhere in the shack, or behind it, a radio was playing.

The Contessa thumbed her horn.

Nobody came to the pumps.

'Must be in the same key as the programme,' said Brad. 'I'll go see.'

He got out and walked to the end of the shack. She saw his head against pale, reflected light. Then he opened a door, and the light was brighter; and the music louder.

He went in.

She heard him raising his voice above the music. 'Hi. Couldn't make you hear. We're out front – need some gas.' There was a pause, then: 'Aw ... gas. *L'auto* ... gas ... *comprenez?*'

'Ah, *l'essence.*'

'You got it, bud.'

The music was quenched. For a moment the Contessa assumed the garage mechanic must have switched off his radio and would be with her in one more moment. Then an announcer began to speak in urgent but, from this distance, unintelligible French.

She released the bonnet catch and, in the glow from the pump by which she had drawn up, got out to check the oil level. As she was about to lower the bonnet again, there was a heavy thud from the shack. Still no-one came to fill the tank; and Brad did not reappear.

The music programme was resumed in mid bar.

Not quick enough and not loud enough to blanket the whine of a car coming along the twisting road.

The Contessa saw the slash of headlights through a sparse thicket. She remembered the turn of the road there, and knew that the car would be passing at full speed or turning in before she could count twenty.

It didn't have to be Harry Rule. But there was a chance it could be. She took out the rotor arm, snapped down the bonnet, and hurried towards the shack.

Just as she reached it, Brad loomed against the light. He was breathing hard, wiping hair back out of his eyes.

The Contessa tried to look past him, but he shouldered his way forward, and they were both outside again.

The sound of the car was closer, matching the jangle of the radio.

'What's that?' Brad demanded.

'Just a car coming.'

'It might be—'

'Might be,' she said.

Headlights raked across the road now, and the newcomer began to swing in towards the pumps. Brad's arm clamped around the Contessa's waist, and he turned her with brutal force towards the back of the building, along to the far end, and cautiously round by a window through whose curtains filtered the same radio programme, the same insistent music.

They stood waiting, motionless, as the Mustang came to a halt a few yards from the Citroen.

6

The first sighting had come from Chauvigny. It was from a *garde-champêtre* who had taken particular note of the car because their village street was so rarely shaken by vehicles travelling at such speed or raising so much dust.

Confirmation of his report came within ten minutes from a wayside inn some few miles south. The proprietor had been leaning in his doorway with the radio going full blast through an open window, and had heard the emergency announcement about the Contessa di Contini and her American companion only seconds before the Citroen slowed on the corner and took the right fork. Yes, he thought the man in the passenger seat had an American look about him. Yes, there was a woman driving. Yes, a very beautiful woman, with a touch of red in her hair. His descriptions tallied.

The reports were flashed to Harry and Paul, cruising aimlessly, mazedly through the Paris suburbs. If word hadn't come soon, Harry would have exploded – or driven, in a moment of fuming inattention, straight into a brick wall. Now he let out one fierce snort, spun the wheel, and headed south-west. Paul began flicking over the sections of a touring map.

'If she's on that route,' he reasoned aloud, his index finger tracing a thin yellow line of weaving roadway, 'she could be heading for Spain.'

'Or for almost anywhere on the Atlantic coast.'

'Hm. But I think they are not planning a seaside holiday. Spain is my hunch.'

'In which case' – Harry was wide awake now, driving the Mustang as though it really were a wild horse, lashing it on between other breeds until they were clear of the outskirts and beginning to go like the wind – 'the road to Toulouse would be a better bet, surely?'

'Too public. And she knows the side roads down Bordeaux

way. Hasn't she got an interest in some *château* outside Bergerac?' Paul watched the lights coming on, headlights flaring and racing towards them. 'Perhaps she is going there, yes?'

'No. Too obvious.'

'Just what she might do, then.'

'You've got something there.' Harry did not slacken speed, but tossed possibilities to and fro in his mind. The Contessa was perfectly capable of driving brazenly to the vineyards and settling into her wing of the *château*, providing Brad Huron with a guest suite, and letting her pursuers scour vast tracts of remote countryside for her.

If Brad let her get that far. If she didn't make a mistake, say a word out of place, alarm him, provoke him . . .

Cold sweat prickled from the nape of Harry Rule's neck down between his shoulder-blades.

He said: 'But then she'd think that *we* might think along those lines, too. It's one hell of a risk. No, I'm betting on Spain.'

'We go to Bergerac first, maybe?'

Still Harry did not slacken. They cut a swathe of quivering light into the swelling darkness. 'No,' he decreed. 'We're too far behind to try any moonlight mystery tours. We've got to play one hunch or the other. And I say Spain. And,' he went on, 'I say we cut out all those side roads – familiar territory to her, but not to us. Maybe beyond Bergerac they're not so familiar anyway. She'll have to get back on to the main road somewhere. So we stick to the highway and get down there as fast as we can make it.'

'And if we guess wrong?'

Harry did not reply. He didn't let that question, which he had already asked himself even as he announced his decision, distract him. Falter now, and they'd be too late anyway. You made a decision; you went through with it. If there had to be a post-mortem later . . .

Again he went very, very cold. Post-mortem: the picture that conjured up wasn't a pretty one.

He thought of the Contessa blithely driving on and on into the night, into the loneliness of the hills. And of Brad Huron maybe getting restless as the hours slipped by; maybe losing the impetus of his jokey assignment and starting to feel that special, deadly hunger of his.

Imperceptibly the speed of the Mustang increased. It thrummed a high whine of protest, but responded gallantly.

They stopped for petrol. Never had the figures on the pump counter flicked over so sluggishly.

'We could be making a mistake,' said Paul as they slid out on to the highway again.

The road began to climb. According to the map there was no turn-off for ten miles. And therefore no slip road in. If the Contessa was on this road, she must surely be on it a long way ahead.

'We could be quite wrong,' said Paul.

'You said that.'

'We could be going in completely the wrong direction.'

Harry's face was set hard. He was not going to let himself debate that possibility. Not now they had come this far.

'We don't know she came this way.' Paul was being a great help – oh, a great moral support! 'Please, I think we pull in to the side and we talk this thing over, yes?'

'I'm saving the talk,' said Harry through his teeth, 'until there's some point in it.'

They took a tight bend and began to tilt down a brief, steep slope. The lights of a filling station gleamed from the roadside. Harry accelerated. They weren't going to need any more petrol for a long time yet.

Then Paul was crying: 'There – that car! It is hers. You see?'

Harry braked hard. They slid in towards the forecourt and he got a quick look at the registration of the Citroen shining back at him.

Not a doubt about it. He felt a lurch of thankfulness in the guts. It was the Contessa's car.

They got out. Paul went towards the Citroen, hesitated, and glanced back at Harry. It was only the slightest of hesitations; but it said more than a string of words. Harry stood where he was until Paul had looked inside the car. There was nobody there – alive or dead.

Music from a radio drifted out through an open door at one end of the ramshackle building beyond the pumps. Watery light spilled out across the lumpy tarmac.

'Let's go see.'

The Contessa and Brad Huron must be almost within their grasp. Had to be. They would hardly have taken to the hills. But he moved warily now. With a bit of luck the jangle of the radio would have drowned the arrival of the Mustang. If Brad and the Contessa were gossiping to some mechanic inside, or maybe asking for some advice on a route, they would find they'd talked too much and too long.

Harry reached the door, tensed, and stepped inside. Paul came close on his heels.

The interior was deserted. A radio stood on a littered bench, singing and moaning on like some senile chatterbox who hadn't realized that her audience had crept out on her.

At the back of the building was another door, a few inches ajar. Brad and the Contessa could have gone out that way. Shown out that way, probably, by the owner or mechanic or whoever had been here.

Harry strode across the concrete floor, and almost measured his length over a huddle of sacking. The sacking was more substantial than it looked.

Regaining his balance, he stooped and pulled one corner away.

Wide, agonized eyes stared up at him from a dead, twisted face. One hand splayed out on the floor, palm upwards, open as though in a last appeal for mercy. A wrench lay a few inches away. There was oil on the young man's denims, but no blood. Brad Huron had a gun with him, but hadn't used it : he had savagely broken the mechanic's neck and twisted it askew.

And by now the Contessa knew what her companion was capable of . . . or had he managed to conceal the killing from her with the sacks?

The two men sprang for the door. They had to run to the end of the building. As they did so, a car engine roared into life.

Harry, incredulous, recognized it. It wasn't the Citroen: the note was that of his Mustang.

They raced out on to the forecourt in time to see it skid over grit and dust, and pull away into the night.

Paul wrenched open the driver's door of the Citroen, and Harry plunged past him. Paul was in the seat beside him as he switched on the ignition.

The engine stayed mute and unresponsive.

Harry jabbed at the throttle pedal, and pulled at the choke, even though he already knew in his bones what the Contessa had done.

'She must have seen us coming,' he said hoarsely. 'She's gone off with the rotor arm.'

They climbed out and stood in the cool of the evening – a pleasant, refreshing coolness which would have been a delight in any other circumstances.

But there was no delight round here right now.

The door of the house at the end opened, and a young woman stood against the light.

Harry said: 'I guess you'd better go and break the news to her. And see if she's got a phone. Pass the word back – and pass it on – anywhere it's likely to ring some bells. We've *got* to get to that nut case before . . .'

The young woman was coming towards them, curious.

Harry left Paul to it and went back into the workshop. He heard a sudden, stifled scream from outside. It made him wince. And then the running footsteps, and the woman sobbing beside him and screaming uncontrollably again as Paul carefully adjusted the sacking and tried to calm her.

She struggled when he tried to lead her away. But Paul's voice had a hypnotic charm even through her despair. She was in a state of collapse; he made her lean on him, and talked and coaxed her out of the workshop.

Harry looked despairingly around. Somewhere in the garage stores there might be an arm which would fit. Somewhere, something to get the engine started. But it was like so many one-man stations: bits and pieces lay everywhere, boxes on the shelves were not labelled, you had to run the place by instinct rather than by system.

There were two motor bikes propped against one wall. Maybe they were in for repair. But maybe the repairs weren't serious – just minor adjustments. Or they could belong to the dead man and his wife, or a friend: crash helmets, goggles and leather jackets hung on hooks not far away.

It was their only chance. He went to the door and looked towards the house.

'Paul!'

The bikes would give them a chance of catching up with the Mustang. Swathed in helmets, goggles and jackets they might get close in without being recognized. And then, somehow, they had to warn the Contessa without arousing Brad Huron's suspicions.

He had just killed that mechanic – perhaps because he had been recognized, perhaps in some fit of uncontrollable anger.

He would think nothing of killing again.

7

The hills made a ragged frieze against the night sky. The Contessa blinked as light dazzled off the flaking white wall of an abandoned cottage – and she found it was the reflection of her own headlights, and had to spin furiously right before they piled up on the corner.

Brad seemed unperturbed. He sat back with his eyes half closed.

All very well for him, she thought. Her own eyes smarted with the need to concentrate on the road, to stay awake.

How many miles before the frontier? And then how many more miles, on over the mountains, before they found a safe place to rest and sort out their programme?

She said: 'Brad, I'll have to stop.'

'Not now.'

'I'm tired. I'm not seeing straight.'

'They're too close behind us.' Irritation thickened his voice. 'They found us. Damn near got us. How'd they find us?'

'They're good,' said the Contessa. 'That's why.'

'Step on it, then.'

'They won't get far without a rotor arm.'

She had told him this before. He seemed to need telling again. And now it worked. He muttered something, chuckled, and relaxed again.

And again she said: 'I'm tired. We go on like this, and we'll finish up off a precipice, or in a concertina against some rock face.'

'We can't stop now.'

'Brad, they don't stand a chance of finding us now. It's lonely up here – we can pull off the road and rest for a couple of hours, and they could go right past without knowing we were anywhere near.'

'I'm not fixing to rest.'

'Well, *I* am.'

She sensed the pendulum of his mood again. He was taut and resentful once more. He had hired her as the expert, yet still he wanted everything done his own way.

He said : 'We've got to make Spain.'

'And we won't make it if I go on like this.'

As though to demonstrate the truth of her protest, a line of trees sprang out of the gloom directly in front of them. She dragged the Mustang to the left, its tyres rasping and juddering along the lumpy verge of the road. There had been no indication of a turn – and wouldn't be on all the other mountainous twists and turns ahead of them.

Brad, jolted hard against the door on his side of the car, said grudgingly : 'OK, so we stop for a while.'

'That inn I had in mind—'

'No. They must have been asking questions all along the road to crowd in on us the way they did. We don't want any more questions. So we stay well clear. Way off the road – right?'

She was ready to agree to anything as a respite for her aching eyes.

'Fine,' she said.

She slowed, dawdling along the narrow road until the lights picked out a rutted lane veering off under the shelter of thick, closely packed conifers. They bumped some forty or fifty yards down it, and turned off again, this time into a clearing littered with fir cones.

When she had switched off the engine, utter silence descended.

Brad said: 'All right. This is what you wanted.' He opened his door and began to get out. 'I'll sit outside.'

'But there's no need to—'

'Make yourself comfortable.' He was, unpredictably, back in his most winsome, boyish mood. It had all become good fun again, as it had been at the beginning – funny, impulsive, a great game. 'I'll keep vigil. That's how it used to be, didn't it, in the good old days?'

'You'll be cold.'

'It's a great night.' He stepped back a couple of paces

and put his hands on his hips, leaning back to stare up into the impenetrable treetops. 'Make yourself comfortable, Contessa. I won't let anybody creep up on us. Not any more.'

She let her eyelids droop. When she tried to open them again, to see where Brad was and what he was doing, they refused to obey her. Weariness seeped up in a slow, sombre wave, and washed over her, lapped her into grateful sleep.

When she awoke, dawn was segments of light between the trees, gashed and splintered and fragmentary; but bright.

Her neck was stiff. She groaned as she turned to look out of the window.

Brad was sitting on the ground with his back to a tree. He stared straight at her. She was sure, somehow, that he had been there for a long time and that he had not allowed himself a wink of sleep.

His unwavering stare was disturbing. She sat bolt upright, and opened the door.

At once he got to his feet.

'Right?' He sounded alert, but not aggressive.

She yawned. 'That's a lot better.'

'You were right.' He waved vaguely, encompassing the whole forest. 'It sure is lonely up here. Big and lonely.'

The Contessa stretched, and wondered whether the forest sported such amenities as a mountain stream. And the usual offices.

She said : 'I'll just take a stroll. Be right back.'

'Big and lonely,' he said again. And when she came back from the shadowy secrecy of the trees, he said : 'I feel free here. For the first time I feel free. They're not going to make me go back.' He stared appreciatively around. 'Not going to make me,' he said fervently. 'Not ever.'

'Make you?' she said, puzzled. 'Who'd want to *make* you?'

He hardly seemed to hear her. Then he forced a grin. 'Why, no-one. No-one's gonna make me.' And the grin hardened, became menacing. 'No-one,' he whispered.

It was cold in this clearing, which the sun would hardly touch for some hours yet, if at all.

'Shall we get going, then?' said the Contessa.

He was like a boisterous, amiable dog clambering in beside her, eager for a treat, eager to be in motion and going somewhere.

She said : 'And once we're over the border, I know another lonely place. Only not too lonely to have a café. I'm starving.'

Brad said nothing, but settled back into his seat; and frowned, and clicked his fingers peremptorily.

They bumped out of the clearing and back along the lane. And they were out again on the road, still climbing.

She was glad they had decided to rest when they did. The convolutions of the road got worse, and if she had tried to press on through the night they would inevitably have come to grief.

A few ramshackle cars approached them from the opposite direction, and a few curious faces peered out : but it was countryside curiosity, nothing unusual about it.

Nothing overtook them from behind.

They struck a busier patch of road outside a small town, and then shook off the traffic as they got deeper into the mountainous terrain.

She wondered, with mocking affection, where Harry and Paul were now. They wouldn't just have sat down on an oil drum at that filling station and given up. Not Harry. Not Paul. But by the time they had rustled up another car, or found a spare part, got themselves on the road again, how could they have hoped to catch her?

She had a vision of them scouring the woods and wildernesses of south-western France, twitching at every Mustang which hove into view, chopping up a map into sections and trying to cover it a piece at a time.

It was hard not to feel sorry for them. She could afford to do so now – now that she was confident she had shaken them off, and could make her own timing and her own terms from now on.

She and Brad would confront them sooner or later. When the bet had been won and there was nothing else to argue about.

A lorry with Spanish markings trundled towards her, and she pulled over to let it racket past.

The villages now were few and far between. And neither specifically French nor Spanish. Here was a rocky, dry no man's land which was any man's land. It made a nonsense of political boundaries.

A white ribbon of road spiralled its way round a peak and came precipitously down to meet them at a cramped intersection. The Contessa slowed, seeing two motor bikes swooping down like birds of prey : black and dizzily swift.

Near the junction they, too, slowed. They were side by side, their front wheels slanted a fraction to the left, waiting for the Mustang to pass before they came out and tore away in the opposite direction.

Blank goggles turned towards the Contessa as she drove past.

The road climbed, teetered along the edge of a vertiginous drop, and then plunged towards a hairpin bend. Just as she hit the bend and slowed to take it without dislodging too much of the road's dissolving rim, she could have sworn she caught a glimpse of the bikes some way behind her.

But the way they had been turned, they had surely been preparing for a run back the way she and Brad had come?

Covering every avenue . . . coming after her now?

She came out on a straight, and slowed down, trying to keep her glances in the mirror casual in order not to alarm Brad. She didn't want to admit he might not get his money's worth – not until she was quite sure.

Far back in the distance, two black shapes on black bikes came bucking into view.

The Contessa pressed her foot down a further fraction of an inch. She wasn't going to panic. It could all be a coincidence, or a misinterpretation. Best, maybe, to slow rather than put the pressure on. Slow, and let the two cyclists pass, and feel at ease.

And if they didn't pass . . . or passed and blocked the way?

Brad was suddenly slewing round, peering back over his shoulder through the rear window.

'Where did they come from?'

The Contessa made a great show of studying her mirror. 'The motor-cyclists? Don't know.'

'They're pushing it hard, by the looks of it.'

'Tourists,' she said, 'out for the kicks.'

She matched her pace to theirs; slowed a fraction. And the men on the bikes slowed. She tried not to give the slightest indication to Brad. But he was too sharp, far too responsive – too clever by half, she thought with growing dismay.

'Why don't they overtake?'

'Waiting for a straight stretch of road, I should think.'

'This is straight enough,' he said.

He was right. But right with a certainty, an almost hysterical intensity, which she didn't like. She didn't like it one little bit. Her own anger at the idea of being outwitted, overtaken by Harry Rule, was nothing like the anger suffusing Brad Huron. To her it was a game to be played for every cent it was worth. And if she lost, it wasn't beyond the bounds of possibility that she'd pay up to recompense Brad for his lost bet. But to Brad it was much more than that: not just a bet, not just a crazy race, one pitted against the other, but a matter of life and death.

Which made no sense. Life and death . . . ? She glanced at his set face; and saw only death in it.

The Mustang weaved across the road.

'For Pete's sake,' rasped Brad. 'What kind of stunt . . . ?'

The Contessa straightened up, attacked a corner full out, and lost the bikes.

But only for a matter of seconds. They slewed round after her, and now the outer one was beginning to close in, swinging gradually out to overtake.

He came level. And rode level.

The Contessa risked a glance. Goggles or no goggles, it was Harry Rule.

He mouthed something at her. She pretended not to notice, but rammed her foot down harder. Slowly they began to draw away. But very slowly.

Brad Huron was leaning forward, staring past her.

'That guy out there . . .'

'We'll leave him behind,' she assured him. 'I can leave him standing.'

'I know who it was,' he said. 'You know who it was.'

'I—'

'Come on, come on,' he snarled.

She admitted defeat. 'It's Harry.'

'What kind of a deal is this? You been keeping in touch, laying a trail of some kind? You figure on getting paid twice, on ditching me and . . . and . . .'

'I'm working for you,' she blazed back. 'Harry's working for your friend.'

'Friend?' His laugh was distorted, discordant. 'Lose them.'

She was still driving, still forcing the pace; but she had given up any hope of winning his bet for him. Harry and Paul must have been up all night, crossing and criss-crossing and cross-hatching the countryside until at last, in daylight, they picked up the trail once more. And that was the way it would be : you would never shake Harry off.

'If it were anyone else,' she said ruefully. 'Anyone else back there . . . anyone but Harry . . .' She shook her head. 'Sorry, Brad. It's no good.'

'I said lose them.'

'And I'm telling you—'

'We'll lose them.' Something hard jabbed into her ribs, so that the Mustang swerved and carved up a few tufts of grass before righting itself. 'And I mean permanently.'

In one glance she took in his face, the beads of sweat, the unstable mouth and all the madness that had at last bubbled to the surface; and the gleam of the gun that was biting into her side.

Hopelessly she said : 'Brad, you don't have to offer that kind of encouragement.'

'Nobody takes me back. Nobody.' He was using the gun as a spur, jabbing pain into her flesh and bone. 'Drive!'

She began to pull away from the motor bikes. And then they pressed it harder, and maintained a distance, and began to creep up again; and she forced it, and screeched round a bend, and wondered when they would meet at last some hairpin bend she couldn't quite get round at this speed.

Sky and trees and jutting rock whirled around her, in upon her and giddily away. The steering had gone crazy, she had lost control and yet was still going. The world and the tottering heavens had all gone crazy. She was being sucked up and out of herself. Nothing mattered any more.

Yet she was driving accurately. The nightmare had nothing to do with the road unfolding in front of her.

She risked a glance at Brad. His eyes were distended. A trickle of moisture ran from one corner of his trembling mouth. He grinned an empty grin at her.

She said : 'You're mad. I ought to have seen it. I ought to have known.'

His acceptance was terrifying. 'Manic depressive,' he agreed. The amiability of it was worse than screaming enmity. 'How do you dig that, Contessa ? A manic depressive paranoiac, with homicidal tendencies. The official verdict.' He beamed at her like a drunkard confiding in his best, most lovingly cherished friend. 'Tendencies . . . I ask you, *tendencies* !' The pendulum swung, and abruptly he was grating : 'Keep going. D'you hear me ? Drive !'

He edged back against the door. Judging the distance between them, slyly alert for any move she might risk, he looked back through the rear window. Then he slowly wound down his own window, propped his elbow on it, and thoughtfully took aim.

8

They saw it coming. Saw the snout of the gun and the edge of his head as he leaned a few inches out. Paul lunged for the left of the road, Harry began to do a slalom down the middle. A bullet shrieked between them. Another spat to the right; a third left Harry's ear singing.

All right, Harry prayed: all right, keep it up, keep on using your bullets up on us. We can dodge, we can outstay you any day.

At what second would Brad Huron's nerve and temper crack: what would make him, finally, turn the gun in on the Contessa and smash them both lethally off the road?

The incline was growing steeper. On one side an outcrop of rock thrust the road out into a series of arcs and loops. On the other, the scrub fell away into a deepening valley. Dodging the bullets became riskier. But Brad's firing also became wilder. And then he stopped, conserving his ammunition.

The Mustang bucked over a ridge in the road and began to descend. There was another, mightier range of mountains awaiting them.

They corkscrewed down into the rugged, deserted valley.

Suddenly dust sprayed up from the back wheels of the Mustang. The tyres screamed, rubber smoke darkened the dust cloud, and the car was lashing from one side of the perilous road to the other. Harry braked, and from the corner of his eye saw Paul riding in close to the rock.

The Contessa must have taken a desperate chance. She brought the car twisting to a halt on the very edge of the unfenced precipice. If Brad turned on her now . . .

Harry ran his bike into the overhang of cliff and let it crash over as he leapt forward, sprawling as he caught the gleam of the gun again.

Brad Huron was nudging open the door of the car. He

was only a few feet from the edge of the drop. He shoved one leg out, braced himself, and threw the door wide open to act as a shield. And dropped behind it, and fired.

Chips of rock showered down on Harry.

Paul made a quick run and flattened himself on the ground a yard or two away. Harry indicated that they should go forward one at a time, keeping a good distance. No need for both of them to get it.

Another shot screeched along the overhang above them.

Harry reached for his own gun.

He called: 'Brad, don't make it worse. We know you're ill. We—'

The wind howled past his left ear.

Paul lunged forward into the shelter of the car's rear wing. There was a pause. Harry waited for the driver's door to open, for the Contessa to throw herself out.

Stillness but for one wayward, drifting spiral of dust which gradually dispersed in the morning air.

Then Brad Huron pulled himself up, craning over the car to see where Paul Buchet had got to. Paul stooped, scurried along the car, and vaulted over the bonnet.

Brad Huron laughed at the top of his voice and swung his gun.

Harry Rule fired.

Brad seemed momentarily frozen by surprise, his shoulder jolting back and then stiffening. He began very slowly to tip backwards.

Paul made a grab. But Brad spread his arms imploringly, his mouth twisted, and he went backwards over the long, deep drop.

Harry dashed for the driver's door and tugged it open.

'Caroline . . . are you all right?'

The Contessa had been sitting slumped forward, as though stunned; or as though unable to look any more, to take any more. At the sound of his voice she shuddered, and put her head back.

'Yes,' she said humbly. 'Yes, I think so.'

He helped her out of the car, and together they joined Paul on the ragged edge of the road. He pointed. Far below, a pitifully small shape was crumpled in a shadowy tangle of trees, scrub and rock.

Harry sighed. It wasn't the way he liked their cases to end. 'Well, I suppose you could say he's won his bet. He's disappeared himself – for good.'

They propped the bikes more securely under the outcrop, where there was less likelihood of some traveller crashing into them. The sun grew hotter on their necks as they pored over the map, spread out on the bonnet of the Mustang.

'Here, I should say.' Paul's finger jabbed down on a thin line of roadway enmeshed in light and then dark blue shading.

'Which means we're only seven or eight miles from that town near the frontier. Somewhere we can find a telephone.'

'And then back to Paris,' said Paul.

'Me, too.' The Contessa sagged against Harry's arm. 'A nice long rest. I can hardly wait. Who's driving back?'

'Paul can go back and tidy up the loose ends,' said Harry. 'We'll hire a car for him in this next place. But *you* are staying right with me, where I can keep an eye on you.'

The Contessa bowed her head repentantly. 'If you say so. But we can all go back together, surely? And you can keep an eye on me very nicely in Paris.'

'I'm not turning back now, when we're over halfway to our next job.'

The sun struck a harsh dazzle from the roof of the Mustang. Paul mopped his brow. 'What job would this be?' asked the Contessa faintly.

'Short memory you've got. Sir Walter Crediton's daughter – it's time we looked her up. And it might help,' said Harry encouragingly, less sternly, 'to have a woman along.'

The Contessa looked appealingly at Paul. Paul looked at her, and at Harry; and shrugged.

She said: 'Oh, well, I suppose it's as restful in Spain as it is in Paris.'

Part Three

THE NUMBERS GAME

I

The telescope panned over the sparkle of the Mediterranean and over the pink and red and brown bodies lying face down on the sand as though stricken from behind by some instant plague. Somewhere somebody was playing a guitar – but it was not the music of some romantic, wandering Spaniard: it came from a cassette recorder hanging from a tourist's shoulder.

A blonde in a primrose yellow costume struggled up from the sand and half turned to survey the white ridge of the promenade. The telescope's eye trapped her for a moment as she twisted her head.

Then there was a click, and she disappeared.

Harry Rule held out one urgent hand. 'Another peseta – quickly!'

The Contessa dropped a coin into his palm and he rammed it into the slot. The delectable girl reappeared, still contemplating the slow drift of tourists and the gleam of cars pulling in close to the beach.

She had the sort of shape which could have been profitably employed advertising almost anything from sun-tan oil to health foods. The more expensive the better. She looked expensive – and lazy, languid and arrogant with it. But worthy of a few moments' aesthetic contemplation.

'Interesting view?' asked the Contessa ironically.

'Oh, so-so.'

The girl thrust one hand down hard on the sand, and her arm stiffened. She was really concentrating on something back from the beach now.

Harry swung the telescope.

A flame-orange MG sports car was parked above the sand. He had already verified that it was hers. And now a Simca drew up alongside it, from this angle seemingly close enough to rip slivers of paint off the panels. An arm reached out of the Simca's window and dropped an envelope on to the seat of the English car. Then the Simca was pulling swiftly away.

The girl on the beach gathered up her towel and a gaudy raffia bag. She adjusted her sunglasses, scrambled up, and began to saunter towards her car. Just as she got in and picked up the envelope, slipping it deftly into the glove compartment, the telescope cut off again.

Harry moved away from it and sat at the table near the edge of the lookout. The Contessa said:

'Nice assignment, hm? Such an interesting girl.'

Harry was touched by the hint of jealousy in her tone. He sat back and relished it for a few seconds.

'Yes,' he said at last. 'A gentleman left her a letter. At least, an envelope. A fat envelope.'

'Containing what?'

'She didn't open it. Just tucked it away and drove off.'

'Then she knows what's in it.'

'Correct.'

'And we'd like to know, too.'

'Right again. And I think it's time we sent a bloodhound out.' He got up reluctantly from the table, where the drowsy warmth was a temptation to forget the world, forget work, forget everything but the sheer warmth and colour and the comfort of being alive. 'I'll start him off.' At the rail he looked back. 'Don't go away.'

'Certainly not. I'm waiting for champagne.'

'At this time of day?'

'At any time of day,' said the Contessa. 'And most especially this time.' She waved him away. 'Go and fire the starting pistol. I'll order a bottle.'

Harry crossed the road, and raised his right thumb. A white Mercedes, too sleek and beautiful to be compared to a bloodhound, slid away from the kerb. It reached the corner as the flame-coloured sports car stopped for a coachload of tourists to turn slowly out of a hotel drive. Harry pointed. The young man at the wheel smiled, his eyes expressionless behind dark glasses, acknowledged identification of the MG, and drove off.

Harry returned to the champagne.

It was cool, and the Contessa was right: this was the ideal time for drinking it. While they waited. He didn't want young Max to let their quarry slip through his fingers; but he wouldn't object if the pursuit just happened to stretch long enough for them to need a second bottle while waiting.

'Nice?' said the Contessa.

'Perfect.'

'I'm beginning to unwind. It wasn't at all a bad idea of yours to come here.'

They drank, and watched the slim bodies and the plump bodies, in and out of the sea, sprawling on the sand or huddling under gaudy umbrellas. Somewhere a car's tyres squealed into a skid. Somewhere a voluble argument broke out. None of it mattered. It was all far away, incapable of shattering the tranquillity.

Harry half wished he had declined to take on Sir Walter's assignment. Right now he was in the mood to sit back and soak up sunshine – and champagne.

'Another glass?' offered the Contessa.

'Why not? They claim it makes your eyes sparkle.'

'It's true. It does.'

'Let me look.'

She laughed, and turned those sultry, feline eyes towards him. He leaned closer. And a shadow fell between them. He looked up to find Max between him and the sun. The blonde girl was beside Max. Their arms were locked in what might have been a loving squeeze if it had not been for the girl's furious expression and the way she tugged vainly to free herself.

Max's free hand dipped into his pocket. He took out the podgy envelope and dropped it on the table in front of Harry.

'That's private property!' blazed the girl.

Harry slit the envelope open. It gaped wide to reveal a thick wad of Spanish currency, wrapped within one fold of a sheet of paper.

Harry said: 'Now let's talk.'

'I've got nothing to say to you. If you don't let me go . . . give me my property back . . . I'll call the police.'

'Go ahead.'

'Who do you think you are?'

Harry said : 'All right, Max. Let go of her.'

The young man relinquished his grip. The girl, her mouth wrenched sullenly sideways, massaged her arm with her other slim hand. She could have run for it; but she didn't. Harry hadn't imagined she would.

'I want that envelope back,' she said.

'Would you like to tell us where it came from in the first place?'

'It's none of your business. I'm not going to stay here—'

'No,' said Harry regretfully, 'it is a bit public, isn't it? Some of your . . . friends . . . might not be too pleased to see you talking to strangers like this.'

'I don't know what you mean.'

'Would you care to join us for a drink at our hotel?'

'No, I wouldn't.'

Harry ostentatiously stuffed the envelope and its contents in his pocket.

The girl looked baffled. He was sorry for her. She was mixed up in something that was already too much for her. But if she wanted to get un-mixed, she was going to have to play it *his* way.

'Do come with us,' said the Contessa pleasantly.

The girl took her sunglasses off for a better look at them. She looked even younger and more vulnerable now, in spite of the autocratic curl of her lips. As Harry stood up beside her, a warm, musky scent came from her throat. She was smooth, beautiful, untouched – and all too ready, he thought, to be contaminated.

'Shall we go?'

Max crossed to the Mercedes and held the door open. The girl looked bitterly from side to side; then got into the car.

At the hotel, the Contessa said : 'Thank you, Max. Send your account to the usual place.'

The three of them went indoors.

It was cooler here, the sun less clamorous through the slats of the Venetian blind.

'Champagne again?' said the Contessa greedily.

'Let's see if we can make a few more eyes sparkle,' Harry agreed.

The girl stood straight-backed and rigid in the middle of the room. 'Why have you brought me here? What's behind all this?'

'Sit down, Susan. You don't mind if I call you Susan?'

She didn't sit down, and she didn't answer his question. 'What do you want?' she snapped back.

'I have a message from your father.'

The full, languorous lips stiffened and tugged down again. 'Oh, him! Well – what is it?'

'Come home. Sounds corny, but all is forgiven.'

'No,' said Susan. 'All is not forgiven. Not that it's any of your business.'

'Isn't it?'

'So he's bought you, too,' she said contemptuously.

'Hired me.'

'Same thing.'

'He *is* your father,' said the Contessa.

'So I should be eternally grateful?'

Really, thought Harry, we do seem to be having a run of difficult children. But this one was not a hopeless case, as Brad Huron had been. This one could be saved. This one he was going to save, whether she liked it or not.

He took the envelope from his pocket. His attitude hardened.

'Right. This envelope. Who's it from?'

'I haven't the slightest idea.'

'I've hit bigger girls than you, baby. Who sent it?'

'Pig.'

Before he could hammer his questions home again, there was a tap at the door. A beaming waiter brought in a silver tray and champagne in an ice bucket. He ceremoniously set three glasses on the table between Harry and the Contessa, and spared Susan one querulous glance as she stood there defiant, glaring her refusal to as much as acknowledge the existence of the champagne. The Contessa jingled a few coins in her hand. The waiter bowed over her, murmured thanks, and went.

Harry said: 'Who sent it?'

'The champagne?' said Susan pertly.

'You know what I'm talking about. The letter.'

'It's from an admirer.'

The Contessa filled the glasses and handed one to Susan, who waved it away.

Harry took his glass and set it beside him. He opened out the paper which had been folded over the banknotes.

'An admirer?'

In the top right-hand corner of the sheet was a cluster of figures which could have been a date, a telephone number, or both; or the sort of menacing sequence of digits you get on income tax forms. Below were neatly written rows of figures:

065872
483009
654888
756533

'Passionate stuff,' said Harry. 'What's it all about?'

'You tell me.'

'I wrote better love letters than that when *I* was a lad.'

'I'm glad I didn't receive them.'

The Contessa said: 'I do think you'd be wiser to answer.'

Harry went to the telephone. Susan tried to maintain her air of defiance but was watching him apprehensively as he reached for the receiver and rattled it in its cradle.

'Who are you calling?'

'I had the British Embassy in mind.'

'Why?'

'I have things to tell them.'

'Why?'

'He'll get them to confiscate your passport,' said the Contessa amicably.

'They can't do that.'

'A British subject consorting with criminals?' said Harry.

'They'll have you hauled in and put on the first flight home. With a lot of questions to be asked at the other end.'

'Who said I was consorting with criminals?'

Harry held up the note and flicked it to and fro. He nodded at the roll of money left on the table by his glass.

'Then what's all this little lot about?'

Susan didn't answer.

The Contessa sipped her champagne and wrinkled her nose appreciatively over it. 'I must say you have more courage than I have. Courage – or something. Getting yourself mixed up in this sort of thing.'

'So long as they go on paying me I'm not complaining.'

'It's a lot of money. What do you do for it?'

'I'm not saying.'

'Sooner or later you will,' said Harry implacably. 'Sooner or later – here, or somewhere else. Somewhere a lot less comfortable.'

She had never been used to such a steady interrogation. Family rows, petulant outbursts, rows with friends and relations and anyone who stopped her doing what she wanted to do – that much you could read in her manner. But not steady, unflustered questioning. She was showing signs of faltering.

'I'm not doing anything wrong,' she said.

'In which case there's no reason why you shouldn't tell us what it's all about.'

'It's private. I'm not supposed to say.'

Harry dangled the receiver between his fingers. 'You've got one more chance.'

She looked at him. He kept his features immobile. She'd find no slackening, no doubts there.

'Oh, all right,' she said. The Contessa held out the champagne glass again, and this time Susan took it with a sheepish attempt at a laugh. 'It was when I first came out here. I was broke. My father wouldn't help. He wanted to force me back home. Plenty of money if I'd play the obedient little daughter, but not a penny if I tried to lead my own life. So I tried to get a job. But I had no labour permit. Then I met this . . . this man.'

'Where?'

'At a party. We got talking, and I'd had a few drinks and I told him about myself, and he said he had some friends who might be able to help. It was easy work, he said, and well paid. But I must never talk about it, or I'd be in trouble – bad trouble.'

'So you chanced your arm,' said the Contessa. 'Who did they turn out to be?'

'I don't know.'

'Come on, come on,' Harry pressed. 'We want the lot. The whole story.'

'But I don't know, really I don't. I never met them.' Her gaze strayed to the envelope. 'Every two or three days I find one of those in my car. All I have to do is take the money . . . and pass on the list of numbers.'

'How?'

'By phone.'

'To whom?'

'I don't know.'

The Contessa appraised her – a woman's sceptical, provocative appraisal, quite different from any look Harry would ever have given her.

'It's true,' cried Susan. 'Look – that sheet – there's a number at the top. That's the number of a telephone kiosk. Then there's the date and time. I have to go to the kiosk at that time and wait . . .'

Harry could visualize it clearly enough. A different phone booth each time, a few seconds' wait, and then a remote voice giving remote but specific orders. Or, rather, the same order each time: just read out the figures on that piece of paper. Then tear it up and throw it away.

'You'd recognize the voice if you heard it?' he asked.

'But it's never the same. Well, not often. I mean,' said Susan, 'I can tell from the operators who butt in every now and then – the calls come from all over. Paris, Berlin, London . . .'

'From London?'

'Sometimes. All over,' she repeated.

Which meant, obviously, an international network. Each

staging post issuing its own directions when it had the tip-off : each distributor waiting for the innocent Miss Crediton to recite the code before setting the highly developed machinery in motion.

Distributor of what?

He had a nasty idea that the nasty, obvious answer had to be the right one.

The figures on the sheet of notepaper danced and jumbled before his eyes. There was no way of interpreting them here. Little Arnold back in London might be able to crack the code. But Harry didn't want to go back to London. Not if the action was here.

Paris, Berlin, London – the real crunch could be anywhere.

He said : 'This latest note. You've no idea what it adds up to? I mean, you haven't got any clues about any of the numbers, or who's likely to call you, after all this time?'

Susan shook her head.

The Contessa said : 'We could try this one out . . .'

'We could indeed. The number for the phone booth, and the time – you *have* to be able to tell us that.'

'Please,' said Susan wretchedly.

'When will they be ringing, and where?'

Harry handed over the sheet of paper. She studied the cluster of figures in the top right-hand corner.

'That'll be the box on the corner of Calle Pedro Silvela,' she said.

'Time?'

'Six forty-five this evening.'

Harry said : 'You'll be there.'

'But—'

'And we'll be there, on the nearest bench, admiring the view.'

'You want me to give them these figures?'

'That's what you've been paid for. Let's leave the account square. But if you get any indication of where the call's coming from, or anything else whatsoever . . . then I want to know.'

'And after that?'

'After that,' said Harry, 'it's up to you whether you want to get deeper in, or whether you want us to get you out of it.'

'I'm not going back,' she said. 'Not to *him*.'

'When you're ready,' said Harry gently. 'When you're ready.'

Unexpectedly, as if something inside her had split open and liberated a part of her which had been imprisoned too long, she smiled a quite spontaneous smile. 'All right. Let's see how it goes.'

At six-forty-five precisely she was waiting in the phone booth, and Harry and the Contessa were sitting under the awning of a café across the street. At six-forty-seven she was out of the kiosk, strolling across to sit at the adjoining table.

'Anything significant?' said Harry, tilting his chair back and contemplating the awning.

Without looking at him she murmured: 'It came through an operator. I heard her say it was London, and hold the line please.'

'London?'

'I read out the figures as usual. And the man was very polite, and he was definitely English. And that was that.'

'London,' said Harry. 'Well, that settles it. We'd better see about a plane.'

2

The curtain in the window twitched. Harry observed it as he got out of the car in the mews and went in through the back entrance of the apartment block. He was not in the least surprised that his own door should open silently for him when he was within three paces of it. And not surprised that it should close behind him with no more than the faintest swish.

'All right, Arnold,' he said admiringly. 'You're getting very sleuthish. But leave the soft-shoe stuff to me. How about your own contribution?'

'I booked the computer time, Mr Rule. For eleven-twenty.'

Arnold was a shy introvert, brilliant when it came to mathematical abstractions but awkward and stammering when it came to the simplest of everyday conversations. He could have devised an excursion trip to the moon and back without his tourists having to allow for more than thirty seconds' delay in arrival back home; but he often had difficulty in getting himself from Wimbledon to Hyde Park Corner.

He stood adoringly back as Harry settled himself at the computer coder set against the inner wall of the office.

'The question is – is this code in our memory bank?' Harry checked his watch, then set the list of figures up before him and tapped them out on the keyboard. When he had finished, he pushed his chair back. He needed a shower. 'Keep an eye on baby, will you? If it's got anything to say for itself, I'll be out in a few minutes.'

When he returned, Arnold was bent over the print-out of the decoder.

Harry leaned over his shoulder.

The pattern was about as helpful as the figures had been: *Savage, fairy, rybstr, albses . . .*

'Doesn't make much sense.'

'Nor the alternative.' Arnold's forefinger, with its bitten nail and flaking skin, indicated the decoder's next attempt: *Morrow, issue, allied, within.* And a third go: *Effect, point . . .*

Harry sighed. He hadn't expected immediate miracles, but he had hoped that some faint indication of a pattern would have emerged.

'I'll leave you with it, Arnold. See if you can crack it. Enjoy yourself.'

He had said it sardonically, but Arnold beamed. He was prepared to do just that. 'Thank you, Mr Rule. Thanks.'

Harry left.

He wasn't looking forward to the next ten minutes or so.

Sir Walter Crediton had the high forehead and slightly thrusting front teeth of a thoroughbred racehorse. He was one of the cold, quiet school of industrialists: he had started as an accountant, and tended to work calculatingly behind the scenes rather than bluster his way into the headlines.

But he was capable of bluster when the fancy took him. It seemed liable to take him right now, as Harry came into his office. He looked past his visitor as the door closed, and said peremptorily: 'You've brought Susan with you?'

'No, Sir Walter.'

'Why not?'

'We haven't got that far yet.'

'What do you mean, you haven't got that far? I want her back where I can control her. I sent you to get her.'

'She didn't want to come.'

'You should have made her.'

'I could have gagged her, I suppose,' said Harry dryly, 'and locked her in a trunk.'

'Why didn't you go to the Spanish authorities?'

'I knew you wouldn't want me to do that.'

'Did you, indeed? Why wouldn't I?'

'When you stopped her allowance, she made . . . other financial arrangements.'

'What has she got herself into now?'

'I wish I knew.'

'You should have made her tell you.'

'She doesn't know herself.'

Before leaving Spain he had at least succeeded in scaring Susan. She had spirit – mixed with a fair proportion of childish defiance – but he had dinned into her that there was a big difference between being happy-go-lucky and being a downright sucker. Whatever she was doing, there was manifestly big money in it. And with that kind of money and that kind of shady dealing, there was danger. Did she really kid herself that she was getting paid just for the sheer music of her voice on the telephone? A girl who slipped easily into a profitable racket didn't, in this wicked world, slip so easily out again.

'I'm not going to dash back into Daddy's arms,' she had said, battling to the last. 'I'm not going to crawl home and fall at his feet.'

'You'd sooner fall into a sewer? Because that's where you're heading.'

'You don't know there's any harm in it. I don't know it myself.'

'But you don't ask too loudly, do you?'

'I get paid—'

'For myself, I prefer to know what I'm getting paid for.'

She was too proud to admit defeat. But with a shrug, as if to say she'd try anything once just for the hell of it, she agreed to play along with them. While Harry was in England, the Contessa would stay put; and if any further cryptic messages came through, Susan would notify her. If the Contessa was out and the pressure got tough, Susan must stall: she was ill, she'd eaten some contaminated *paella* – *something* . . .

And if she never got another call? If someone was wise to Harry Rule's intervention and to the Contessa poised there, waiting? Or, worse, prepared to remove Susan Crediton before she spilled too many more words?

Don't panic, said Harry to himself.

To Sir Walter he said: 'She's a pawn in some dangerous game.'

'And what exactly are you proposing to do about it? I engaged you—'

'To get her back. And you'll have her back. But maybe not tomorrow, or the day after. Because when she does come back I want to make sure there'll be no nasty follow-ups.'

Sir Walter's basilisk gaze had probably given many a junior executive a dose of nightmares. But before Harry Rule's stern face, his own gaze dropped.

Quietly he asked: 'You have any . . . any plans at all?'

'As far as she's concerned, nothing. Not for the moment. Not until I know more about her associates.'

'Mr Rule, she's my only child. I am relying on you.'

Harry got up to leave. 'You keep on doing just that.'

He returned to his apartment office.

Harry had a tidy mind. His methods were, on the whole, tidy and methodical. Even when he acted on impulse, on sheer intuition, it was somehow controlled by an inner censor as scrupulous as the Recording Angel.

Arnold, though meticulous as a mathematician, could create more chaos about himself in a couple of hours than the most romantic poet in the most decrepit garret. He had succeeded, in Harry's absence, in making Harry's well organized office look like a stationer's shop hit by a typhoon. Papers were scattered about the floor. He had scribbled notes on the blotter and even, in a moment of what Harry hoped would prove to be inspiration, on a patch of white wall. Reference books were heaped up like a circulating library's clearance sale. From the middle of a thicket of crumpled paper snaked the telephone flex. Arnold was saying:

'Um. Ah, yes. At what time is that? Um.' He made a note on the nearest unblemished sheet which came to hand. 'Uh-huh. And the number is six . . . three . . . eight. Right? Yes, that checks. Um. Thank you.'

He replaced the receiver and turned a meditative gaze up towards the ceiling.

Harry allowed him somewhat more than a minute, then said encouragingly: 'Come up with anything, Arnold?'

'Well,' said Arnold, slightly ruffled at being disturbed in

the middle of his trance. 'Yes. I think so. Having considered all the alternatives, I personally fancy the first group. You know . . . this one.' He scattered sheets of paper like a flurry of falling leaves, frowned, and then plucked the original print-out from the débris. ' "Savage" here eludes me,' he confessed modestly. 'But assuming that "fairy" is in fact "ferry", and assuming that the letters "PM" in the third group indicate time, then the figures immediately ahead of—'

'Er,' said Harry. 'I mean, please, just the answer, huh?'

'The answer?' Again Arnold looked put out, but rallied. 'Well, again assuming that we return to the original numbers where we are not using the coded letters . . .'

Harry stopped him with a look. Arnold's respect for Harry overcame his religious awe at the beauty of what he had revealed. He tore off the bottom of a sheet which he extracted from the pile, and said crisply:

'In ordinary terms, I'd recommend a watch at Dover. And if there should be a car coming off that particular crossing with registration ALB 638, then you might get some results.'

'Thank you, Arnold. Sounds a lot simpler put that way.'

'I didn't want to have you thinking it was all that easy, Mr Rule,' said Arnold with a coy, engaging grin.

3

The Contessa paid the taxi driver and hefted her bag out on to the quayside. A hand darted down upon its handle.

'Carry your bag, ma'am?'

'It's all right, thank you. I'm waiting for . . .'

She looked at the man. It was Harry. His car was drawn up behind him. With a graceful flourish he swung the case towards the open boot.

'I thought you were never going to make it,' he said.

'I thought the same,' she said tetchily. 'One mix-up after another, all along the line. The way I spurred that driver on, he must have thought I had a demon lover right behind me.'

Harry glanced over her shoulder and shook his head reassuringly. 'Must have lost you at the last crossroads. Well – what news from Spain?'

'They've passed the girl another message.'

Harry whistled gently. 'That means they don't suspect anything.'

'But she's there, and we're both here.'

'Yes. What did you tell her to do?'

'To go ahead. I thought it was safer than exposing her – leaving her on her own to face whatever they might dream up.'

'Right. But the moment we can clear things up here, we'd better get back fast.'

'And as a matter of interest,' said the Contessa, 'why are we here? What are we doing at Dover?'

'We're not here for the fish and chips.'

When it came to fish and chips, she thought, the Costa Brava probably had more establishments to offer than Dover or, indeed, anywhere on the English coast. This hasty scurry across Europe didn't much appeal to her. She was about to state her somewhat petulant case when Harry opened the door of the car and signalled that she should get in. When she was settled, he handed her his binoculars.

A giant hovercraft was racing in towards the harbour, skimming on foam and appearing to breathe a dewy haze against the bright sky. She lost it for a moment; then it was filling the lenses.

'Who's aboard?'

'Wish I knew,' said Harry. 'The computer came up with several alternatives. This is one of them.'

'And you've dragged me back all this way . . .'

'I can see us having to think fast. Split up. Chase off in opposite directions, maybe.'

'Or maybe nothing.'

'Maybe nothing,' he conceded.

'But you can't cope without me.'

Harry hesitated. Then, with a sigh of gentlemanly surrender, he allowed : 'I don't know I could manage without you.'

The hovercraft rose like a vast white bird in a ruffle of plumage, then slowed in a swirl of foam. It sank again and headed for the concrete apron.

'This seemed the surest bet,' Harry said. 'If there's a car aboard with the registration ALB 638, it'll all seem a whole lot surer.'

The hovercraft spun, tilted, and settled on to the apron. The howl of its engines died. Half a dozen dark figures ran across the concrete. Harry sat back, his head against the window, looking past the Contessa.

Without taking her eyes off the 'bird' – like a swan, so graceful afloat, so clumsy ashore – she handed his binoculars back to him.

The doors opened and the cars began to roll off.

Harry thumbed the focus, getting the registration plates as large and close as possible without blurring them.

A couple of Jaguars came off, followed by three cars with French and Belgian plates. Then a Cortina camouflaged in luggage and plastic sheets.

And, swimming into view, the numberplate : ALB 638.

Good old Arnold. A wizard. A genius.

'A Rolls, no less,' Harry murmured.

They watched it come off. Waited for it. Not a difficult car to spot, or to follow.

It was a surprisingly leisurely journey. Once they were on the M2, Harry would have expected the driver to light out as hard as he could go for London. People who've got through Customs with anything hot have a tendency, he'd discovered, to put their foot down once the way is clear. Exuberance or the desire to shed the stuff – either way, it made for speed. But the Rolls was purring contentedly along at just under sixty.

'Whatever he's up to,' the Contessa observed, 'he's not going to be rushed.'

Not too close, James, said Harry to himself. He was a lot more impatient than the man in front. The driver of the Rolls knew where he was going. Harry didn't. The suspense was killing him.

He looked up in the driving mirror. Other cars pulled out, passed him, passed the Rolls.

There was a station wagon which could easily have done the same. But it was holding back, taking it easy. Every now and then it pulled very slightly out to assess the traffic ahead, then slewed back into line. Whatever other cars sprinted forward or nipped into a vacant slot, the driver adjusted his own speed and placing to keep no more and no less than four cars between himself and the Rolls. The fact that Harry and the Contessa were in one of these didn't seem to have attracted his attention. Or, if it had, he was doing nothing about it.

Suddenly the Rolls, slowed for a mile or so behind a long trailer, swung out to pass. The station wagon leapt out as though a trigger had been squeezed, anxious to maintain its distance.

Harry cast an apparently idle glance at the driver as he drew level. The man was young and lean, with a swarthy face and shining black hair. He could have been Italian; possibly Spanish. He did not spare even a brief look for Harry.

A faint but urgent note began to bleep from the dashboard.

'Come in, Arnold. What is it?'

Sibilant and faintly pinched, Arnold's voice said: 'I've traced the registration, Mr Rule. It's a Rolls-Royce.'

'I know.'

'You know? You mean it's actually there?'

'Right in my sights,' Harry assured him. 'Now, who's the owner?'

'It's registered in the name of Savage.'

'Have we got anything on him? Any record of any kind?'

'This,' said Arnold, 'is Lawrence Savage – of Harley Street.'

The Contessa felt Harry's jolt of surprise.

'Doctor?'

'An eminent heart surgeon,' said Arnold.

The Rolls was in keeping, thought the Contessa. The rest of it wasn't. Had the decoder come up with a way-out piece of guesswork? Did its circuits need the attentions of a surgeon?

Harry was saying: 'D'you have his home address?'

'Out beyond Chelsfield. The Old Barn, Quarry Lane.'

In due course the Rolls turned off towards Sevenoaks. The station wagon discreetly followed suit. Harry put his foot down and overtook both of them. The Contessa flipped over the pages of a route map and said: 'There ought to be a railway bridge a mile ahead. We could take the right turn up a B-road there, and get to the place ahead of them.'

There was a railway bridge. Harry took the right turn.

They found the Old Barn at the end of a lane flanked by widely separated, expensive houses. On the crest of a ridge were the last stragglers of the London suburbs. Here was a little hamlet in itself, a rich man's viewing platform on the edge of lush, rolling countryside.

There was a turning-place at the end of the lane, sheltered by flowering shrubs. Harry drew up in one cranny, just out of sight of the main stretch of lane itself.

They got out. The Contessa leaned against the car and surveyed the melting, surging, interwoven shades of green falling away below her and then climbing again to a whale-backed hill. Twilight steeped the valley in a darker hue, its shadow slowly climbing the far slope.

Harry stood close to the corner, by a high slatted fence, and looked out along the road.

They had fifteen minutes to wait before the Rolls came into sight. It slowed and turned in between the wrought iron gateposts. The Contessa began to edge forward, but Harry's hand on her arm restrained her.

'There's the boy to come yet.'

As he spoke, the station wagon nosed round the far end of the lane. It drew to a halt under a lamp standard nearly opposite Savage's gate, just as the light came on.

There was a pause. Then the young man got out and sauntered across the road, hands in pockets. He had disappeared into the house approach when a door clicked; and abruptly he was coming out again, easing back into the shade of the hedge.

Someone began to whistle tunelessly. With a shrug of despair, the pursuer made a detour back to his station wagon, out of sight of the gateway. He slid back into the driver's seat, and wound down the window.

The whistling went on, and there was a steady hissing accompaniment.

'Now what?' asked the Contessa.

Dusk welled up through the trees and shrubs. A man with a frisky poodle came out of one of the houses and set off for a stroll in the opposite direction.

Harry murmured: 'Do you have an envelope in your bag?'

'Filling in the time, writing letters to the old folks at home? The light's not too good. Bad for your eyes.'

'You don't have to write a letter. Just so long as you post it.'

'A tactful way of subsidizing the Post Office?'

'Take an envelope,' said Harry, 'and walk to the post-box on the corner.'

'If there's one there.'

Even as she spoke, she remembered glimpsing the red

shaft of a pillar-box as they turned off the road into the lane.

'There's one there,' Harry confirmed. 'Now. You're tasting the evening air, going to post a letter. Take your time.'

'It won't go till morning, anyway. Not now.'

'That's not likely to occur to Hawkeye. To him you'll just be part of the scenery. Very convincing, actually : a typical product of this neck of the woods.'

'Thanks, I'm sure.'

'Off you go, then. And find out what's going on along there.'

The Contessa took an envelope from her bag, sealed it, and carried it ostentatiously in her left hand. She strolled a few yards in the shadows and then came out under one of the sparse street lights, hoping it would look as if she had emerged from the house immediately to her right. She put on an act of musing, tilting her head back, sniffing honeysuckle drooping from a hedge, and then staring meditatively down at the ground.

When she drew level with Savage's house, the hissing noise was excuse enough for her to glance, shaken from her reverie, up the drive.

A man in blue trousers and shirtsleeves was hosing down the Rolls.

The Contessa went on as slowly as she dared. A few moments before she reached the pillar-box, the noise ceased. Instinctively she made a move to look back; but restrained herself.

There was the slam of a door closing, crisp and loud on the still air.

She put the envelope into the dark maw of the box, and risked a quick check on the lane.

The young man was getting out of the station wagon again. His head turned towards her. She made a show of trying to read the collection times listed on the panel of the pillar-box.

In a flash he had darted across the lane, and vanished.

As she began to retrace her steps, Harry came in fast and silently from the far end. They met at Savage's gate. Harry edged round one post and moved, crouching, up the few yards of drive.

There was a light on in the garage beside the house. At any moment, presumably, the chauffeur might come out to polish the Rolls and finish the job.

The young man was already on his back, wriggling under the car. The Contessa stood in the shadows as Harry closed in on him.

A flashlight flickered under the dripping body. It wavered, went out. The young man wriggled free.

And Harry, gun in hand, knelt beside him. The Contessa could just hear his whisper.

'Thank you. I'll take that.'

There was a gasp. Harry's free hand reached forward. A small, dark container was placed in it.

Suddenly the front door of the house opened.

'Down!'

The two men huddled close to the side of the Rolls as a tall, distinguished looking man with silvering hair came through the brightly lit opening. He pulled the far door of the car towards him and leaned in to take something off the seat. Then he went back indoors.

The chauffeur began to roll back the garage door.

Harry must have jabbed his gun into the young man's ribs, for there was a brief grunt; and then the two of them were hugging the shadows and escaping out into the lane.

'Take this.' Harry shoved the gun at the Contessa.

'You cannot do this. It is not . . . I will call the police . . . I will—'

'You won't,' said Harry.

The Contessa prodded the young man on his way towards their own car.

'I do not know who you are.' The accent was plaintive and almost certainly Italian. 'You have no right . . .'

Plaintive and protesting it might be; but he was keeping his voice down. And he allowed himself to be nudged towards the car and into the back seat. The Contessa got in beside him while Harry, in the front seat, took a screwdriver from the shelf and tried it on the lid of the metal box.

'No, you must not.'

'Look here, Giuseppe—'

'I am not Giuseppe.'

'Then who are you?'

'I will not say.'

'Then you'll remain Giuseppe to us.' Harry turned the container on its side and began to chip at the sealing material which ran all the way round. 'What's inside?'

'I do not know. But please, no, you must not break that seal.'

'Not going to go off, is it?'

Giuseppe, or whatever his real name might be, sagged back despairingly against the seat.

The Contessa kept the gun unwaveringly on him, but peeped over the front seat as Harry chipped the seal away. There was a squeak as the two halves of the container came apart. Inside was a cellophane packet. Harry pierced the side with the screwdriver, and tipped a few grains of white powder into his palm. He tasted them warily.

'Heroin.'

'No!' cried the young man extravagantly.

The Contessa's lip curled. 'Surprised?'

'Sure, I am surprised.'

Harry swung round in his seat and gave him a long, hard look.

'I am saying nothing' – Giuseppe or Giovanni or Marco or whatever, he was trembling and trying to sketch denials in mid-air with his long fingers – 'nothing until I have seen my lawyer.'

Harry reached back and opened the door. 'Out.'

'You are letting me go?'

'On your way.'

'You are not the police?'

'That's right.'

The young man looked helplessly at the Contessa.

'But . . . I can't, it is not possible.'

'Why not?'

'Is not possible,' he repeated dolefully. 'I do not deliver that, I am in big trouble.'

'Tough,' said Harry unsympathetically.

'Please. I beg you. Give it back to me.'

'Who are you supposed to deliver to?'

'I do not know.'

'What a lot of things you don't know!'

'Please. I swear it.'

Harry pushed the door as wide open as it would go, and put his hand on Giuseppe's shoulder as if to heave him bodily out.

'All right, all right. Please. I tell you.'

'That's better.'

'I wait at a public phone box. They call. They tell me where to park the car. I leave the car with that' – he indicated the container – 'on the seat.'

'And when you come back it's gone.'

'And there is money in its place,' said the Contessa.

'Sure. Is like that, like you say.'

'Now you can go.' Harry pushed hard this time, bundling him out.

'But no. I can't. You do not understand.' He gripped the edge of the door, swung imploringly round it towards the Contessa. 'Please. They will kill me.'

'You were ready to gamble in a very dirty game,' she said implacably. 'So. Now you've lost.'

'Please.'

'You've got one chance.' Harry dragged the door clear of his fingers and shut it. He started the engine, and said: 'Keep running.'

They left him with his dark features paling, raised in anguished prayer under the lamp at the end of the lane.

4

The tangy aroma of steak diane swirled up from the sizzling pan and began to drift through the apartment. Sniffing rapturously, the Contessa pursued Harry into his gleaming kitchen. He worked dexterously, deploying his culinary skills as professionally as his investigatory ones.

'A cagey lot,' she observed. 'They take no chances. Planting their dope on innocent cars and leaving respectable citizens to run it across the border for them.'

'All over Europe.' Harry nodded, with a tinge of what might be reluctant admiration.

'They don't even risk making the phone calls themselves.'

'We'll get to them.'

It sounded fine. She said dubiously: 'What's the next move?'

'We eat. Then we start finding out where they planted that container on the Rolls. Nice and unobtrusive, stuck underneath like that. But who did the sticking – and where?'

They ate. The meal was perfection. The Contessa would have hated to pit herself against Harry in a cookery contest. It was infuriating, really. He was too infernally good at everything. Just once, in just one field of activity, she wouldn't mind him falling flat on his face.

But the steak was perfect. No use denying it. She inhaled a cool breath through the spicy warmth; and a fragment of meat went down the wrong way. She began to cough. Harry leaned over and patted her on the back. She clutched her chest, coughed, and tried to speak. The words came out sore and rasping.

Harry poured a glass of wine and handed it to her. Gradually the convulsive coughs subsided, but her heart pounded for a few minutes.

When she could speak coherently, she said: 'I need a doctor.'

'You'll be all right in a minute. Just take it easy, have another glass—'

'Medical advice,' she insisted. 'I need a specialist's opinion.'

'On what?'

'My palpitations. My heart.'

'It's the first I've heard of . . .' Harry chewed a mouthful, stared at her, and then began to grin. 'Of course. I'm with you. Yes, I do think you ought to see a qualified man. No sense in letting these things run on until it's too late.'

'That's what I thought. A good night's sleep—'

'And then,' said Harry, 'you'd better run up and down stairs a few times. Or run all the way to Harley Street. Just so he'll get a convincing demonstration.'

'For all we know, he'll have a long list of appointments. May not be able to see me.'

In fact when she telephoned in the morning, Savage's receptionist did make it clear that there simply wasn't a moment to spare for the next three or four days. Mr Savage had been away for three weeks, he could not possibly fit anyone else in. Perhaps an appointment a fortnight from now . . .

The Contessa di Contini was very upset.

The Contessa di Contini? The receptionist was sorry she hadn't really heard the first time. It was just possible . . . by a little bit of rearranging, Mr Savage might be able to see the Contessa. Would eleven o'clock be convenient?

Eleven o'clock would, the Contessa assured her gratefully, be ideal.

She did not run to Harley Street, but walked more briskly than usual. And she made one quick circuit of the block before ringing for admittance.

Savage was charming. His bronzed face brought out an intense blue in his eyes – a twinkling, rich blue which matched his club tie and gleamed as delightfully as his smile.

He examined the Contessa, made reassuring noises, and asked a few questions – questions she had known he would ask, and to which she had all the answers ready.

'You mustn't worry about this condition,' he concluded.

'Such palpitations can be distressing at the time, but they're not dangerous. They act as a sort of alarm signal, telling you it's time to slacken off. You're really in excellent health.'

The Contessa adjusted the emerald pin on her jacket, and smiled. 'That's a relief.'

'They may be caused by an anxiety state. I'll prescribe a tranquillizer. If the symptoms recur, do come and see me again. But for the time being, I think that perhaps if you can persuade yourself to unwind . . .'

'I *was* thinking of taking a holiday.'

'Excellent. You do that.'

'You've been away recently yourself,' said the Contessa casually.

'How did you know that?'

'Your handsome suntan.'

Savage touched his cheek with a fingertip and nodded reminiscently. 'Ah, yes. I was down in Spain.'

'Lucky man. Where were you?'

'On the Mediterranean coast.' He scribbled on a prescription form. She waited, hardly daring to probe further. Then he added : 'A place called Cabannes.'

'I don't think I know it.'

'There's a delightful hotel there, with its "feet in the sea", as the French say.'

'I may try it one day.'

'I recommend it.' Savage held out the prescription, and shook hands with her. 'Its therapeutic value is incalculable.'

The Contessa left, and reported back to Harry.

'Cabannes?' he said. 'Right. Let's go and treat ourselves to some more sunshine.'

'But will they use the same place twice running?'

'Whatever the breadth of distribution once the stuff is in Europe, it has to come *in* somewhere. And there must have been a reason for choosing one particular place of entry.'

'There could be several.'

'There could be,' Harry agreed curtly. 'But we have to start somewhere. And I have a hunch—'

'Oh, Cabannes it is, then.'

When Harry had a hunch, there was no point in arguing. She could only hope they wouldn't have to sit around for days, or even weeks, wasting their time.

5

Wasting time. It was beginning to look like that.

Harry sprawled on the balcony outside his room and tried to persuade himself that the rest was doing him good. It did a man no harm to put his feet up and let the world go by for a little while. Reinvigorated, he'd easily be able to catch it up when he wanted to.

But it didn't come naturally to him. The Contessa seemed able to switch off at a moment's notice, lie back, and soak up as much sun as the heavens cared to pour down on her. Not Harry Rule. His metabolism didn't function that way.

He got up and leaned on the rail.

The hotel certainly had its feet in the sea. The foundations ran sheer down into a ragged sprawl of rocks, with the water lapping and streaming round each outcrop. A speedboat went out in a wide white flurry, and waves surged in over the rocks, sprang skittishly up towards the restaurant terrace, and fell away again.

Tucked away behind the building was the car park. He wondered if anyone was in there yet. Probably not, in broad daylight. Yet it was a simple matter, a matter of a few seconds. They would have to go on keeping their vigil, just in case. A moment's inattention, and another package might be on its way without their knowing.

He looked at his watch, and turned back into his room.

They might be anywhere. Might be running the stuff in at any one of half a dozen chosen places, ringing the changes, working out their own permutations according to yet another code which he'd have to get his hands on.

Wasting time. Keeping a watch here while, for all he knew, consignment after consignment of drugs was speeding on its way towards England, Holland, Germany and heaven knew where else.

He went down the corridor to the Contessa's room, and knocked.

'Who is it?'

'Me. Harry.'

'Come in.'

He found her lying with her head blissfully back in the sun slanting down on to her balcony. Within the shade of the room, a case was propped open on a chair. As Harry squatted beside her, he saw yet again the picture of the car park which was already engraved on his mind.

It was one of Paul Buchet's neater devices. A slowly panning eye scanned the car park, keeping even the remoter corners in deep focus. You could keep watch day in, day out, without ever setting foot out of doors.

The trouble was, the standard of the programme wasn't in the highest order of entertainment. After an hour, your eyes began to ache. After two hours you'd have been happy to see every automobile in the world go up in flames. Anything to break the monotony.

A man came into shot. The Contessa pushed herself up on her elbow. Harry tensed.

The newcomer got into a BMW and drove decorously out of the park.

The Contessa lay back.

'Enjoying yourself?' growled Harry.

'Could be worse. But I think we're wasting our time.'

'Maybe we should call Susan again.'

'I did it. An hour ago.'

'And?'

'She's had no messages for three days.'

'That ever happen before?'

'Once there was nothing for a week.'

'Then let's not spread despondency. Maybe they're just resting. Waiting for a new batch.'

'Or,' said the Contessa, 'they think they've had a fair run for their money with Susan, and they're dropping her. Using somebody else.'

The thought had been nagging away in his own mind but he had tried not to listen to it.

'You can close your eyes now,' he said. 'I'll take over for a couple of hours.'

'I'm all right.'

'You need a rest. You can do the evening session, and I'll take over for the night.'

He took the compact television screen back to his room, drew the shades, and settled in front of it. That evening he had dinner for two sent up, and the two of them talked without looking away from the screen, as though hooked on some terrific tennis duel or the closing hours of a golf championship.

When the Contessa had gone to bed, Harry poured himself a large whisky – but not large enough to make him somnolent – and settled down for the rest of the night.

The shapes of the cars in the park were only hunched shadows now. He had to concentrate, letting no shift of light or misleading splutter on the screen distract him.

He ran a hand across his eyes, rubbing the ache into the corners.

Something moved.

He blinked. Little red blobs and cobwebby strands gashed his vision. But there was no doubt that, through and beyond them, someone was sliding between the bonnets of the parked cars.

His right hand stabbed out automatically. The buzz from the pocket-size transmitter awoke the Contessa, and he heard her sleepy voice:

'Eh . . . mm . . . yes, what is it?'

'It's me.'

'Aw.' She yawned. 'What is it?' she demanded again.

'The fish are biting. There's someone down in the car park.'

'Back from some late-night flamenco?'

'Not the way he's moving.'

The shadow blocked the screen and then wandered on. A subdued light at the entrance to the park struck an echo from a polished panel. Harry's eyes narrowed. The man creeping between the vehicles stopped, and swung something forward in his hand. He was standing by a car whose registration number was indecipherable; but even in the uncertain glow Harry could make out the single bold letter 'B' in a white ellipse. A batch due for Brussels, Ghent, Antwerp, Liège, then?

The figure sank and disappeared. Harry leaned forward, longing for some supernatural control that could blow the picture up to ten times its present size and at the same time dig into the blackness to extract just what he needed to see.

In blackness there was a deeper blackness. The man wriggled out from under the Belgian car, looked round, and hurried towards the perimeter of the car park.

Harry was out into the corridor, down the deeply padded stairs without waiting for the lift, and out of the side door which he had already noted. The flitting shadow was out on to the quiet slip-road, on its way to the junction past which some late drivers still raced or meandered.

Then it veered to the left.

There was a flight of steps down to the strip of sand beside the rocks. From here you could walk under the shallow cliff to the village – a village still intact and secretive, despite the overbearing growth of hotel and promenade and garish restaurants so close to it.

The man who had crept in and out of the car park was walking towards the village. Not too fast, but with a loose, easy-going stride. A man with a weight off his shoulders – even if that weight had been no more than a pound or two.

Harry hugged the contours of the cliff. Ahead were a few lights, pallid and spasmodic. One went out as he cautiously approached.

Fishing boats were pulled up on the asphalt hard above the beach. Beyond was a single line of shops and cafés. In the daytime they would be festooned with gaudy, pathetic souvenirs, relying for trade on those tourists who felt they would get something more authentic here than in the plushy arcades opposite the hotel. At this time of night they were bare and shuttered.

Another light winked and went out.

Harry's quarry wove a path between the boats and plodded over the hard towards a café amounting to little more than a scrofulous plaster archway with double doors. Tables and chairs clustered in front of it, their umbrellas collapsed like flags when the wind has dropped.

Harry waited in the shelter of a boat. He saw the man fumble at one of the doors. It opened, he went in; it grated shut behind him. There was the thud of a bolt being rammed home.

Allowing a good three or four minutes before moving on, Harry ambled past the front of the café. The name above the door was short and decisive enough : PEPE.

He made a circuit of the village and went back along the clifftop path to the hotel.

There was one prediction he was willing to make : the Belgian car would be leaving immediately after breakfast.

It did just that.

'And we let it go?' said the Contessa.

Harry sipped his orange juice. 'I'm not concerned with nailing down the odd delivery van. I want to shut the gates on the marshalling yard.'

'So?'

'So we have a mid-morning drink in one of the picturesque village cafés.'

'The wine can be terrible.'

'We'll stick to coffee.' Harry rubbed his stinging eyes. 'It may help to keep me awake.'

The scene was so warm and welcoming and different by daylight. The shop frontages blossomed. Silence exploded into a hospitable babble. Harry, wearing his loudest shirt and a cravat which made the Contessa wince, led the way up to Pepe's double doors. Alone among the neighbouring establishments, they remained shut.

Harry pounded his fist on one of the tables. '*Ola!* Señor Pepe!'

It took five minutes to rouse the proprietor. A rattling and shaking at the bolt heralded his appearance, bleary-eyed and apologetic.

'*Buenas dias . . .*' His eyes shuddered against the sun. '*Y que dia! Estupenda.*'

Harry nodded agreement. '*Dos cafes con leche, por favor.*'

'Pronto. Pronto.'

As Pepe went back inside, the Contessa said: 'That's him?'

'That's the man.'

The double doors swung loose, revealing an arched room within. Along one wall was a coffee machine, and behind the bar a row of bottles. A smell of last night's dregs wafted out into the sunlight.

The Contessa said thoughtfully: 'I have an idea. One that should cause the maximum panic and confusion.'

'Good. Tell me.'

'Every time he places a container under a car, we take it.'

'That was the idea, eventually. But it'd be better to—'

'We take it,' the Contessa pursued, 'here and now. On the spot. Before it gets moving. And we empty it, and re-seal it – and put it back again.'

'Put it back?'

'Think of the angry blasts there'll be from all over Europe. And then the man at the top will be forced to show his hand.'

Harry contemplated her, awestruck. 'Caroline,' he said reverently, 'I love you.'

It was a reasonable cue for her to lean closer. Really, in this setting, in this light, she was just too ravishing to be true. If Harry concentrated on her as effectively as he was accustomed to concentrating on his job . . .

The dream was shattered by Pepe, rattling cups and saucers down upon the table and ogling them. If they wanted to convey the impression of being a couple of amorous trippers, they were certainly succeeding.

'Thank you,' said the Contessa sweetly.

'It is a pleasure.' Pepe balanced a tray on one hand, swung a coffee pot from it with the other in a flourish as magnificent as that of a matador coming in for the kill; and poured. 'On a day like this it is good to be alive, eh?'

'Yes,' said Harry. 'Yes, it is. Good to be alive. We should make the most of it.'

When Pepe had gone, the Contessa said: 'A pity that Belgian one got away before I thought of this.'

'There'll be plenty more,' said Harry.

'I hope so.'

When they got back to the hotel there was a message from Susan Crediton. She had received instructions, to be carried out the day after tomorrow.

Business was looking up.

6

The first container they intercepted in Cabannes was taped under an Audi destined for Frankfurt. It was followed within twenty-four hours by a package meant for Paris. Then there was a lull, broken by Pepe in the small hours of a Friday morning when he brought two batches to the car park: one for attachment to another Belgian vehicle, one finding its way beneath an Aston Martin. Each time the cars were due to leave the following morning. Pepe's contacts within the hotel must be pretty reliable.

And each time Harry and the Contessa got to the packages before departure. Swiftly they removed the cellophane packs of heroin, re-sealed the empty containers, and sent them happily on their way.

After the fifth, the Contessa observed: 'They'll be taking up panic stations any time now.'

'Um.' The job done, Harry wanted to go to bed. 'They'll be pulling Pepe in.'

'They'll take him to the big man?'

'There's bound to be a sort of area manager. He'll want to grill him himself.'

'He'll risk being seen by Pepe.'

'No risk. When you're taken to the man, you don't come home again.' Harry yawned. 'Better get some sleep before we go for our usual cup of coffee.'

'Do we have to?'

'Yes,' said Harry, 'we have to.'

By now they knew the name and markings of every boat on the beach, and the hues and designs of every straw hat and plaited basket on the stalls. But they dared not miss a morning. When the balloon went up, this was the likeliest launching pad.

A few hours later the Lamborghini was on its way along the cliff-top road. They brought the car every day now, short as the distance was. No telling when a fast blast-off was going to be called for.

The Contessa was showing the strain. She wore dark glasses not to shield her eyes from the sun but to disguise the bruised heaviness caused by hours of watchfulness.

They drank the usual coffees; and made them last.

Nobody else showed up until lunchtime, when a group of Pepe's cronies drifted in from the village, and loquacious arguments seethed up. It was all part of the daily rhythm – cheerful, innocuous, undisturbing.

Harry and the Contessa left. And returned next day. And the next.

This time they were greeted by a muffled explosion from within the dark cavern of Pepe's café. The Contessa, starting to sit down, gripped the edge of the table and silently consulted Harry.

He faced the dark doorway. Surely nobody would rub Pepe summarily out, right on the premises?

Pepe himself emerged, beaming. He was carrying two glasses and an ice bucket, which he set down on their table.

The ice cubes tinkled merrily round the neck of the bottle.

The Contessa stared. 'What's this, Pepe? We didn't order champagne.'

'It is a . . . what you say . . . a *regalo, señora.*'

'A present? How nice. But what have we done to deserve it?'

Pepe drew the bottle from the bucket and twirled a napkin stylishly round its neck. 'You have done such honour to my little café. Every day you are here. Is pleasure to see you. My very best customers.'

He poured champagne. Sunshine was trapped, bubbling, in the glasses.

'A charming gesture. Thank you, Pepe.'

Harry was about to add his thanks when he saw that Pepe's smile was going sad around the edges. The bottle remained tilted in his hand, dripping slow, cold drops on to the table. He was looking beyond them.

A car had stopped by the end of the souvenir kiosks. In the front sat two men with tight curly hair and dark glasses.

One of them leaned an elbow on the door and gave Pepe a curt nod.

'Perdón, señor . . . señora.' Pepe's voice was strangled. He let the bottle clatter back into the bucket, and went to call into the café interior. 'Maria! *Venga abajo, por favor.*'

Then, his lips slack and quivering, he went towards the car. It was like watching a man on the eight o'clock walk from the death cell.

Once he had slumped into the back seat, the car reversed violently, spun on a patch of sand, and roared off through the village.

Harry was on his feet. 'Get back to the hotel. Switch on – right?'

'Right.' The Contessa was already grabbing her shoulder bag and turning towards the cliff path.

'And stay put. Don't leave until you hear from me.'

'Don't keep me waiting too long.'

'I have a feeling it won't be long,' he promised.

He raced for the Lamborghini and wrenched it round in as impressive a cloud of sand as Pepe's visitors had achieved.

Off the main coast road there was not a lot of traffic. And far ahead, just visible, the car which had snatched Pepe away was obviously abandoning the coast road.

It began to climb. Closing the distance between them, Harry also began to climb. The road surface deteriorated; and it hadn't been too good in the first place. At least it had one advantage: even when the car ahead disappeared behind rocks or into dark patches of stunted trees, its dust haze was easy enough to follow.

The tell-tale cloud slowed. Harry took it easy round a tight bend, and saw a high, castellated wall ahead, broken only by a formidable medieval gateway. There was an echoing blast from the horn of the car now edging into its shadow. The gates opened, and Pepe was taken inside.

The gates closed on him.

Harry pulled in to the side of the road. He climbed the bank, and could just see over the wall to the squat shape of an old, stone-built house, almost a fortified manor house.

He hesitated. But squatting here would achieve nothing;

going back to Cabannes to have a lengthy discussion with the police wouldn't be any too good for poor little Pepe's health; and in any case that wasn't why he had driven up here in the first place.

Frontal assault: nothing like it, nothing so good for the adrenalin flow.

Harry went back to the car and drove up to the gates. He sounded his horn.

One wing of the gates was tugged open a fraction, and a man with a drooping black moustache peered out.

'Open up,' said Harry confidently. 'The *señor* wishes to see me.'

'I am sorry. I think he does not wish to be disturbed.'

'Just you tell him I want to talk to him about registration plates. English, Swiss, German, Belgian. He'll understand.'

The man backed away to an alcove in the wall and took up a phone. Harry watched him. He watched Harry. At last he put the phone back and came out to drag the gates wide open.

'The *señor* will see you.' Before Harry could drive on, he added in a shout: 'Giovanni!'

A heavy-jawed man with lowering brows emerged from a small lodge behind the entrance. Without a word he slid into the seat beside Harry and nodded once.

Harry proceeded up the drive to the miniature fortress ahead.

The main door opened as they approached. He crossed a hall rich with the glow from a stained-glass window over a wide staircase, flanked by Giovanni and the man who had been waiting inside the door.

Another door opened. Within was a book-lined study. Giovanni indicated that Harry should enter, and followed him through. The second guard backed away and closed the door behind them.

'How kind of you to call.'

The man behind the huge desk was in his middle forties. He had hard, dark eyes, but his manner was urbane, faintly quizzical. His accent was impossible to identify. In appearance Italian, he had a trace of something more Central

European – and something else which suggested he had mixed a lot with Americans, or spent some time in the States.

'As I was passing,' said Harry airily, 'I just thought—'

'But I am afraid I don't understand your message.'

'It's very simple. You're worried. I came to put your mind at rest.'

'That is kind of you, Mr . . .?'

'Rule.'

'Mr Rule. But I was not conscious of having any worries.'

'Well, first, Mr . . . *Señor* . . .?'

He heard the rustle of a footstep behind him. He could sense Giovanni shifting his weight, poising for an attack if ordered.

The man behind the desk sucked air thoughtfully through his teeth, then said : 'Giocometti. No reason why you should not know it. No reason at all, since you are here.'

The menace in the last few words hung in space, a sword over Harry's head.

'First, then,' he said, 'there's no point in your leaning on Pepe. He's not responsible for your loss.'

'Who is Pepe? And what have I lost?'

Harry took one of the plastic bags from his pocket and tossed it on to the desk.

Giocometti was a cool customer. He inspected it curiously, without the slightest flicker of alarm.

'What is this?'

'Found it under a car,' said Harry.

Giocometti's pitch-black eyes were raised. An eyebrow was raised. He looked to one side of Harry, and nodded calmly.

Giovanni drew a gun.

'That won't help,' said Harry. 'It would be a bad mistake.'

'The mistake was yours in coming here, Mr Rule.'

'Well, I've got this impulsive streak.'

Harry moved his hand slowly towards his pocket. Slowly, because he knew the silly things that could happen when trigger-happy bodyguards took fright too soon. Giovanni swung the gun towards him. Harry smiled reassuringly, and took the small microphone from his pocket.

'Receiving me loud and clear?'

'I wouldn't say that,' the Contessa complained. 'A bit squeezed, before.'

'We can always use some filters and boost the tape through an amplifier.'

Giocometti's expression became less complacent, more baleful. He glared at the microphone as though it were a live thing.

'And now,' said Harry, 'would you please convince Señor Giocometti that this is not the killing season?'

'One moment.' As Harry turned the tiny two-way radio towards the desk, the Contessa went on: 'I wonder which branch of the family it is? Mario Giocometti, or Paolo? Neither of them has too savoury a reputation in Rome, as I recall. Much safer living in Spain. Let me see – Paolo's the Tuscan. Nearly six feet. Mario, five foot eight, a bit of a gash between his eyebrows—'

'Mario,' said Harry.

'Then, Mr Mario Giocometti,' said the Contessa, 'let me assure you that I know Mr Rule is with you, and I shall expect him back here in the next twenty minutes. Oh . . . and, Mr Giocometti, I shall expect to see Pepe with him.'

Giocometti got slowly to his feet, both hands thrust down against the desk. He looked at Harry. Then, with a growl, he dragged open the two top drawers of the desk and snatched a brief-case up from the floor beside his chair.

Harry watched amiably, Giovanni blankly, as Giocometti stuffed papers into the brief-case and then crossed to the far wall. He opened a safe, began to add bundles of notes to the contents of his case.

'Hope you make it,' said Harry.

Giocometti snapped the catch shut and took three paces towards the door.

'You can run,' Harry continued, 'but for how long? A day . . . a week . . . a year? We're not going to keep quiet about this, you know. I've got a lot of talking to do to the police. And' – as Giovanni questioningly raised his gun again – 'if anything unpleasant happens to me, you get murder added to your problems, and the Contessa hot on your heels. And I tell you, she'd never let up. Never.'

The brief-case dragged Giocometti's right arm and shoulder down.

He said : 'What is the alternative?'

'Spain, or Italy, or wherever they finally find they've got jurisdiction over you – they've all got some equivalent of States evidence. Give it a thought.'

Giocometti looked at the door, so few feet away. Then he dumped the case, and turned back to his desk.

Harry nodded. 'There's a good boy. And when you've finished with the phone, may I use it?'

He had a call to make to young Susan Crediton. To set her mind at rest. And at the same time to persuade her that her father, too, had a mind which should be set at rest.

He had a hunch that she would be a whole lot readier to listen now than she had been such a short time ago.

Victor Canning

THE SCORPIO LETTERS 30p

'Crisp thriller ... the mysterious blackmailer Scorpio is excitingly and violently unmasked.' – DAILY EXPRESS

THE GREAT AFFAIR 35p

'A first-rate adventure story ... high on action' – BOOKS AND BOOKMEN

THE MELTING MAN 30p

'Few more macabre settings for a climax could be imagined than the private waxworks of a mountain chateau ... Crisp, polished and as tense as they come.' – BRISTOL EVENING NEWS

QUEEN'S PAWN 30p

'Canning at his best ... a master of invention and suspense.' – TIMES LITERARY SUPPLEMENT

MR FINCHLEY DISCOVERS HIS ENGLAND 35p

'This is a quite delightful book, with an atmosphere of quiet contentment and humour that cannot fail to charm.' – DAILY TELEGRAPH